Deadly Institution 2

Holly Copella

To Aunt Janet & Uncle Kerwin

ACKNOWLEDGMENTS

Copella Books: First Paperback Edition 2016
Cover Artist: Daniela
SelfPubBookCovers.com/Daniela
Printed by CreateSpace, An Amazon.com Company

PUBLISHER'S NOTE

Chapter One

The Stony Ridge Country Club was nestled on a large hillside estate along the outer edge of the small, quiet town. The private club was a playground for the wealthy and had every amenity to pamper its elite clientele. There was a large outdoor pool, an indoor exercise pool, numerous hot tubs, his and her spas, tennis courts, and, naturally, an eighteen-hole golf course. Prior to being transformed into the luxurious club, the building was a thirty-year-old summer mansion in desperate need of repair and it was considered an eyesore for years. For the last three years, the country club had been a breathtaking sight even to those who opposed its presence in the small town. Within the evening setting, every light remained lit both inside and out, giving an awe-inspiring view to those within town.

A neatly dressed man in his late sixties, Doyle Cobbler, walked along the empty main hallway while heading toward the back office area. Doyle was a tall, slim man with a full head of thick, white hair.

"Mr. Cobbler," a woman called from behind him.

Doyle turned and saw a young woman in a tight, black dress with daringly high heels attempting to jog to catch up with him. She was Lea, the hostess from the Men's Smoking Lounge. She waved a piece of paper as she slowed her approach.

"I have a message for you from your secretary," Lea announced while handing him the paper. "She called about five minutes ago. I was just on my way to your office to put it on your desk."

He accepted the paper.

"Bridget said she's going to be thirty minutes late for your eight o'clock meeting this evening," Lea informed him while attempting to smooth out her dress from her brisk jog.

Doyle gave her a puzzled look then glanced at the note. "I wasn't aware that we had a meeting scheduled for this evening," he remarked then shrugged. "I suppose Bridget would know. Must've slipped my mind." He glanced at his watch. It was a little after seven o'clock. "That still gives me plenty of time to take a steam." He looked at the attractive, young woman and smiled. "Thanks, Lea."

"Certainly, Mr. Cobbler."

"Pretty quiet around here for a Saturday evening," he remarked.

"Tonight is the museum gala," she replied simply then offered a polite smile. "I'm surprised you and Mrs. Cobbler aren't attending the party. I hear half the town is going to be there to welcome the new scientists."

"Oh, the gala," he announced then shook his head. "I completely forgot." Doyle grinned then chuckled. "Davis felt the board members should skip the gala in silent protest. My wife felt differently and planned to attend on my behalf with Davis' daughter. I suppose I should have remembered when I saw Jeannette was all dressed up before I left."

"I hope Mrs. Cobbler and Miss Lowe enjoy themselves at the party," Lea chirped then grinned while sweeping a glance of admiration over the older, handsome man. "Enjoy your steam, Mr. Cobbler."

Lea then turned and hurried back to the smoking lounge before she was missed. The lounge was probably equally vacant tonight, and the young woman was almost certainly bored out of her mind with little to do. Doyle watched her leave with more than a passing interest. He glanced at her backside in the tight dress and grinned his approval. Although somewhat flirtatious as part of her job, Lea wasn't as easy going as her sexy dress suggested. A man holding a thick pocketbook wasn't enough to lure the young woman into his bed. Not surprising, there was an actual list naming the easy women working at the club and the wealthy male members had it memorized. Most of the better ones weren't cheap either and none worked for free. Welcome to the boys' club. Just another scandalous institution for the small town.

†

The elegant all wood steam room was three levels of stadium seating surrounding a mound of large rocks, providing steam throughout the room. Doyle entered the steam room wearing a white towel wrapped around his waist and one draped across his shoulders. Despite his age, he was psychically in excellent shape, although his light coating of chest hairs were mostly white, and he had more hair on his shoulders than he used to have. He poured some water onto the large rocks, causing them to hiss and send a wave of steam across the room like a rogue fog. He made himself comfortable on the first row bench and spread out. It wasn't often the steam room was empty and certainly never on a Saturday evening. Having the steam room to himself was a rare treat. He leaned back onto the second row of seating and placed the second towel from his shoulders over his face. As he soaked in the excessively warm, moist steamy room, he heard the door open but didn't bother to remove his towel to see who had entered. He was used to others coming and going.

The bench alongside him creaked as someone joined him. It seemed odd with the entire room empty that someone would sit so close. Doyle removed his towel to have a look at his fellow member. A kitchen knife slashed firmly across his throat. He barely managed a surprised gasp as blood poured from his neck and down his chest in a small waterfall, rapidly soaking into the white towel around his waist. He clutched at his throat then lifted his eyes to look at his attacker. His eyes widened with horror then rolled back. He collapsed onto the first bench as his blood continued to spill from the slit in his neck and across the elegant, wooden bench.

†

The men's spa was void of life as was most of the country club that particular Saturday evening. Soft music filtered through the hidden wall speakers to drown out the gurgling sound of the sauna tub.   Within the glorious twelve-person hot tub, a woman in her mid-thirties was partially submerged in the center of the churning, bubbling tub.   Her eyes were open, seemingly staring at the ceiling. Her lips contorted, conveying her last moments of life, possibly gasping for her final breath.   Even in death, Bridget was beautiful. On the table alongside the hot tub was a scotch glass and a half-empty bottle of vodka.   An empty bottle of sleeping pills gently rolled on the table near the glass.   The discarded kitchen knife stained with blood was partially hidden within a white, blood-soaked towel.   It lie on the floor near the hot tub steps.   A soaked piece of paper floated in the water near the dead woman.   Scribbled on it were the words, 'if I can't have him, no one will'.

Chapter Two

Three months later. Not far from the Stony Ridge Country Club was an exclusive development lined with large, expensive homes on well-kept, landscaped yards. Beyond the mammoth entrance to the wealthy community was a moderately dark home. Although it was only a little after nine o'clock on a Sunday night, it appeared as if the occupants were either out or already in bed.

The large master bedroom was only dimly lit by a low burning fire in the gas fireplace, lending a romantic glow to the quiet bedroom. Two empty wineglasses set on the nightstand alongside the enormous, kind-sized bed. A woman in her late twenties, Jeannette Cobbler, slept peacefully beneath the slightly rumpled sheets covering her naked body. Her long strawberry blonde hair was mussed, perhaps from her wild evening. Something interrupted her slumber. She slowly woke feeling disoriented and looked around. The mass beneath the sheets alongside her didn't stir. Jeannette slowly sat up, allowing the sheets to fall from her naked, toned body. Her full, large breasts were too round to be natural, looking more like two large cantaloupes than actual breasts. She slipped out of bed and into her discarded, slinky satin nightgown, which was lying on the floor with other scattered clothing. Without care for her bare feet, she padded across the room for the open door.

Jeannette walked down the elegant grand staircase to the broad foyer below. She shivered from the excessively cool air on the first floor. Despite being late summer, the night seemed particularly chilly. Perhaps she'd left a window open. She turned the banister and entered the grand hallway heading toward the kitchen. She paused before the open study doorway and peered into the darkened room. For some unknown reason, she entered the study and flipped the light switch along the wall just inside the doorway. The study brightened considerably. She looked around as if expecting to find something, but nothing seemed out of place. The study was as elegant as the house itself with heavy, antique furniture, towering bookcases, and a small bar not far from the excessively large desk. Something on the desk caught Jeannette's eyes.

She uncertainly approached the desk while staring at the small object on top. As she got closer, she realized it was a small flashlight. She stared at the flashlight a moment, appeared to consider its reason for being there, and then glanced across the room. The study appeared empty. She approached the desk while studying the flashlight then eyed the desk drawers. One of the metal locks contained fresh scratches. Jeannette immediately became alarmed and pulled on the drawer. It was unlocked! She gasped softly then reached for the desk phone. Jeannette was suddenly grabbed around the waist from behind, pulled against her assailant, and a black gloved hand covered her mouth to keep her from screaming. Her assailant breathed against her neck.

"Where is it?" a male voice demanded then removed his gloved hand from her mouth to allow her to speak.

"Where's what?" she gasped with a quiver in her voice.

"Don't fuck with me," he snarled softly. "Tell where it is or I'll snap your neck."

Jeannette hesitated and carefully considered her response. "It's in an envelope in the bottom drawer near the back," she gasped softly.

The man thrust her onto her knees, keeping a firm grasp on her wrist, and opened the bottom drawer. He routed around the back of the drawer, found a thick envelope, and felt the contents through the outside. He released her wrist, grabbed her by the hair, and forced her to look up at him. He wore a black mask, so his identity remained hidden. He pulled a hunting knife and held it to her face. She let out a frightened scream.

"Next time, you won't be so lucky."

He released her hair and punched her on the side of the head. She fell to the floor and was unable to move, dazed by the hard hit. It had only been a matter of minutes before Jeanette was able to open her eyes and look around the room. She slowly pulled herself to her feet and held her head with some disorientation. The man was gone, but it wasn't much comfort.

Chapter Three

On the beautiful, sunny Monday morning, the small airport, which was only an hour from Stony Ridge, was alive with travelers being dropped off for their flights. A man and woman walked together toward the terminal entrance and paused outside the automatic doors to say their farewells. Jacey McMurray was an attractive woman in her early twenties. She wore a business casual black skirt and jacket with matching pumps. Her long auburn hair was pulled neatly back into a French twist of sorts. Stray locks of hair seemed to fall haphazard from the twist. Jacey was the fresh-faced girl next door, who seemed almost as out of place with her purse as she was in her uncomfortable pumps. Dr. Maxwell Alvord, on the other hand, looked at home in his expensive suit. He was a moderately handsome man in his early thirties with short dark hair and a clean-shaven face. He carried a soft, leather briefcase containing his laptop and business papers. As they faced each other, the tension between them was obvious.

"I have meetings all afternoon and then that dinner this evening, so I won't be back until after midnight," Maxwell reminded her.

Jacey nodded mechanically and refrained from fidgeting, although she felt herself shifting from foot to foot. Of course, that could be because her feet already hurt.

"So Brian will pick you up tonight?"

Maxwell nodded. He studied her expression, inhaled deeply, and appeared equally uncomfortable. "I know this is all happening rather fast," he announced as he gently took her hand in his and caressed it. "I love you, Jacey. This job in Denver is an amazing opportunity. You'll see."

She tensed slightly while staring into his eyes. Jacey wasn't certain how to respond to this 'amazing opportunity' that he kept referring. He fidgeted and looked at his watch, indicating he had to check-in. She didn't want to send him off with an argument. She gently squeezed his hand and forced a smile.

"I know it's important to you, Maxwell," she replied. "We can discuss it tomorrow."

He seemed reluctant to release her hand and refused to take his eyes off her. "I meant what I said last night," he announced. "I want to marry you, Jacey." He tensed slightly. "You never really gave me an answer."

Her entire body stiffened as she stared into his eyes. "You didn't exactly ask," she replied while fidgeting. "We have a lot to discuss. This is a lot to take in on such short notice. I need time to think about everything that's happened." She gently pulled her hand from his and patted his chest. "Go to Denver and impress your new boss. We'll talk about our future tomorrow after I get out of work."

Maxwell offered a warm smile and nodded. "I'll call you tonight before my dinner party."

"Call me at work," she replied. "I have a lot to do after work, and I won't be near the phone."

He nodded. Maxwell gently touched her face and kissed her briefly but passionately on the lips. She returned the kiss and again fidgeted before smiling.

"Have a safe trip," she announced warmly.

He returned the smile then entered the terminal. Jacey waited a moment then felt her smile fade into a frown.

"Damn it," she cursed softly then headed toward her parked jeep.

✝

Later that morning, the Stony Ridge Country Club was alive with golfers and carts at nearly every tee. Men and women dressed in their finest golf attire seemed more interested in conducting business and gossiping about fellow golfers than the actual sport. The outdoor pool was mostly empty for the early hour, although it would be packed later in the day with children of club members. A few members dined on coffee and pastries on the patio overlooking the lush grounds while awaiting spa appointments, golf tee times, and various lessons. The interior of the club was more impressive than the outside with rich, detailed woodwork, marble floors, and stained glass windows.

Jacey entered a large reception office through a set of antique looking doors with frosted glass. The reception office was more of a small lobby. It contained two secretary's desks belonging to Jeannette and herself. Both were positioned outside the office doors on either side of the reception area. The office to the right belonged to Davis Lowe, the country club president, and the one to the left belonged to Nathan Stanley, the vice president. Jacey glanced at her watch and tossed her purse on top of the desk with disgust. She anticipated being late and had notified her boss, Davis, to the fact, but she didn't intend to be two hours late. At least her boss didn't mind. He knew she was dropping Maxwell off at the airport for his business trip to Denver.

Fortunately for her, Maxwell knew Davis from years ago when he worked in the city. Maxwell used his influence with Davis to get her the coveted position as his executive secretary. Although Jacey had been working full-time with her position at the library and writing articles for the local newspaper, she couldn't refuse the salary associated with the new position at the country club. It wasn't her dream job, but it provided greater financial freedom. She collapsed into her chair and stuffed her purse into the bottom drawer. Her first order of business was to see what messages were left from the weekend before the phone started ringing, which was due to happen shortly. She picked up the few notes left on her desk from that morning.

The first note was gut wrenching. Davis' chicken scratch across the paper read, 'Jeannette called in sick'. Jacey groaned and allowed her head to hit the desk. The message should have included the word 'again'. Jeannette was out more than she was in. Her recently deceased husband, Doyle, had left her enough money that she really didn't need to work, which reflected in the amount of time she'd spent out of the office. It wouldn't be a big deal if it didn't double the amount of work Jacey then had to do. Manning the two phones would be enough to keep her busy most of the morning. As both phones rang almost simultaneously right on cue, Jacey dreamed of riding her horse through a quiet pasture. It seemed a farfetched dream while trapped in her office hell.

Chapter Four

The Garden Room was the less formal restaurant within the country club. The room was large and airy with white, wooden furniture and, much to its name, contained a lot of plants and flowers. It also had seating outside on the terrace overlooking the massive country club garden. The Garden Room was a favorite for elegant tea parties, sweet sixteen parties, and general meetings for many of the club wives. Some fondly referred to it as 'the hen house'. It was now nearing one o'clock and the favorite lunch spot was moderately busy for a Monday. As Jacey sat uncomfortably at the round table with her two lunch dates, she was reminded of how much she didn't belong in the snooty dining area. Most of the women having lunch or tea, as they liked to call it, were dressed in their flowery best. All that was missing were the large hats. Jacey rarely ate within the club restaurants but had little choice when she had lunch dates. Fortunately for her, her lunch dates always treated, which was good since she probably couldn't even afford a cup of tea at the country club.

The two men at the table with Jacey were almost as out of place in the room as she was. Professor Ted Fuller was a tall, lanky man in his early to mid-thirties with dark hair and wire-rimmed glasses. A studious looking man, he fidgeted a great deal in the chair that seemed too short for his long legs. His counterpart was a robust man with wild, curly black hair and shifty eyes that took in everything happening within the room. Dr. Timon Bennett was easily in his mid-thirties, although mentally, he was a big kid. It was almost hard to believe both were renowned scientists. She'd met both men a little over three months ago, along with Maxwell, their colleague. They'd come to town with a few other scientists on a mission to convert the old Stony Ridge Mental Institution into a museum. After several major setbacks and a scandal or two, the old mental institute was finally shaping into a fine museum. How their relationship got to where it was today was a whole *other* story.

"It's been brutal with Jeanette out sick today," Jacey announced with a weary sigh.

Her friends were sympathetic to her bad morning, although it was possible they knew more than they led on.

"As much as she calls out," Professor began, "you'd think her boss would have let her go by now."

"Maybe he would, if he wasn't sleeping with her," Jacey remarked matter-of-fact.

Both men seemed surprised by the comment.

"Really? Jeannette and Nathan?" Professor questioned in a pitch higher than usual. He gently cleared his throat and resumed his more masculine tone while attempting to sound less like a busybody. "I never would have suspected."

"Well, it's just a rumor," Jacey replied and sipped her tea. "I probably shouldn't spread gossip, but it's difficult not to in this place." She eyed several older women around the room then lowered her voice. "It's like a gossip freeway."

Timon was unusually quiet. Normally, he would have added his two cents by now.

"Huh?" Timon finally remarked, so as not to disappoint. "I wish I'd known she was of easy virtue sooner. I would've asked her out." He casually leaned back in his chair and glanced around the room, noting the old women staring down at him. He then spoke louder than necessary. "For the most part, this town is overflowing with old busybodies and virgins."

Professor glared disapprovingly at Timon.

Timon chuckled at the look he was given then glanced at Jacey. "No offense to the virgin at the table," he teased.

Professor placed his hand over his eyes and groaned softly while shaking his head.

Jacey felt her cheeks redden slightly. "None taken," she muttered.

Telling the guys her sexual status was possibly the biggest mistake of her life. Timon enjoyed teasing her relentlessly about it. Although, she did tend to take cheap shots at him when opportunity presented itself as well.

"Besides," Jacey replied, swiftly changing the subject, "I doubt you could afford Jeannette. She doesn't even have to work. Her late husband was Doyle Cobbler, the board member who'd died three months ago."

Both men stared at Jacey with shared looks of surprise. She knew what they were thinking before either even spoke. The age difference was staggering.

"Wasn't he an old man?" Professor nearly gasped.

"Yeah, like, really old," Timon proclaimed, catching the attention of every white haired woman in the lounge.

Professor kicked Timon under the table, causing him to yelp and jump.

"Sorry," Timon gasped softly.

"He was in his late sixties," Jacey replied simply. "Almost forty years her senior."

"Didn't I hear something about that being a murder suicide?" Professor asked.

"That's what the homicide detective called it," Jacey replied then sighed. "It's hard to believe Doyle was fooling around with his secretary. I guess when he wouldn't leave his wife; she killed him and then took her own life."

"I vaguely remember that. Didn't they find her dead in the hot tub in the men's spa?" Professor asked with a curious tilt of his head.

"Yeah, she took a bunch of pills and drank half a bottle of vodka," Jacey replied. "They didn't find either of them until after midnight." Jacey grimaced slightly. "Apparently, after several hours, the heat and moisture really did a number on the bodies."

Professor and Timon grimaced.

"Did you know that happened the same night as the museum gala?" Jacey asked.

"Must've been a full moon," Timon muttered then looked back at Jacey. "Bet he left his wife a fortune, huh? With his share of the country club and all, she'd be set for life."

"Actually, when an investor dies, their portion of the club reverts back to the surviving investors," Jacey informed them. "She didn't get any part of the club."

"Explaining why she moved on to investor number two," Professor replied while hiding his sly grin.

"Well, there had been a rumor that she was having an affair even before her husband's death," Jacey remarked while raising her brows in suggestion.

"Maybe she and her lover offed her husband," Timon teased and released a throaty chuckle. "This town is like Peyton Place. Stranger things have happened."

"Yeah," Professor muttered while shifting in his tiny chair, "and we were up close and personal with more town scandals than I'd care to remember."

"Speaking of scandals, lies, and false allegations," Timon teased cheerfully while looking at Jacey, "when's Asher coming home?"

Professor again groaned softly at Timon's idea of a joke, although his friend didn't seem to notice or just didn't care who he embarrassed.

"Poker night just isn't the same without the rich guy with no luck," Timon continued.

Jacey shifted in her chair. "Four days, six hours, and counting." She held back her laugh. It wasn't as if she were counting down the minutes until her friend's return, but she couldn't deny she missed him terribly. "I never knew house sitting plants could be so exhausting. And now that my mom and Russell left on yet another trip, I have to look after the farm, my horses, and Asher's jungle sized garden."

"You know, you could always ask Maxwell to help," Timon remarked.

She fidgeted and became uncomfortable by the suggestion. She was well aware that both men watched her. Maxwell may have been their colleague, but they knew something wasn't right. They were both just too polite to bring it up.

"Maxwell still has trust issues with horses and even more with Asher," Jacey finally replied, although she knew they knew what was going on in her relationship with Maxwell. Denial was a game they were playing for the sake of peace where all were concerned. "I wouldn't bother asking."

There was an awkward silence and it seemed as if none of the three intended to address the issue once again.

"Things still not better with Maxwell?" Professor finally asked, breaking the rules of the 'don't ask' game.

She hesitated and considered her answer carefully. "I'm afraid he's reverting back to his old scientist ways," Jacey informed him then cast looks at both men. "No offense to the other scientists present."

"None taken," Professor replied.

"You don't act all stuffy and pompous," Jacey remarked then hesitated. "Neither did Maxwell when we first met, and it's only been three months. I don't know what's up with him."

"Missing the city life," Timon casually replied. "Doc doesn't exactly pay well. But, it's still better then dealing with those high society types."

"You're standing in the middle of snob central," Professor interjected while glaring at his odd friend. "What are you talking about?"

"Yeah, but this is small-town snob central," Timon bluntly informed him. "These snobs are like the white trash of the elite society."

Jacey laughed and stood. Both men stood also.

"I really need to get back to work," Jacey informed them. "I came in late and took an executive lunch on top of that. It doesn't bode well with the powers that be." She then proceeded to hug both men. They eagerly returned the embrace. "Thanks for lunch, guys."

"Anytime," Professor replied then studied her a moment, leaving an awkward silence. "Are you unhappy here, Jacey?"

She shrugged, attempted a smile, and refrained from being honest with them. "It's a job," she replied then hesitated. "Nathan's been in a mood lately. I'm just tired."

"Once the museum is complete," Professor announced, "we'll probably need someone full-time in the office. I know Doc would hire you, if he knew you were interested."

"Yeah, and we'd save a fortune on membership dues hanging out at this dive," Timon remarked.

Jacey stared at them with surprise. "You mean you'd give up your membership if I didn't work here?"

Professor shrugged and smiled timidly. "It's not really us," he remarked.

"We just come for the scenery," Timon teased and grinned his true meaning.

"You're wonderful friends, and I appreciate the offer," she replied while holding back her laugh. "When the day comes, we can discuss my relocation. For now, I should probably get back to work while I still have a job." She groaned softly. "I probably missed a hundred phone calls already."

"We should probably get going anyway," Professor informed her.

Both men grinned and simultaneously placed cigars in their mouths.

"We have massages scheduled with Ingrid and Ursula," Timon announced cheerfully through the cigar clenched in his teeth. "I love a butch Amazon woman."

Jacey hid her smile to their boyish grins. She was lucky to have them as friends.

Chapter Five

Jacey entered the reception area to the sound of her phone ringing with its usual sense of urgency. She hurried toward her desk, snatched the phone from its cradle, and immediately heard a click. She groaned softly and slammed down the phone. Nathan's office door opened. Three men dressed in expensive suits exited the office while laughing like old friends, despite that they barely tolerated one another. It was the club's worst kept secret.

"I assure you," the first man announced in a jovial tone. "The security cameras can't be shut off without triggering the fire alarm. If someone is screwing around, it's going to be caught by security."

"There goes your chances of getting lucky in the elevator," the second man teased the third man.

There was another round of laughter. Whatever perverse fantasy the three men had been laughing about came to a sudden halt when they noticed Jacey seated at her desk. The three expensively dressed men were the country club investors and board members.

Essentially, they were the men who owned the country club. The first man was Davis Lowe, Jacey's boss and president of the country club. Davis was a pleasant looking man in his forties. Although not excessively handsome, he was easy on the eyes. His hair was prematurely gray for a man of his age. The second man was Nathan Stanley, the vice president. Nathan was ruggedly handsome, taller than Davis, and had the build of a man who spent hours playing racket ball. Although in his early forties, he looked much younger than Davis. His neatly trimmed, golden-brown hair didn't have a trace of gray; of course, it was possible he colored his hair. The third man was Carl Wexler. A moderately meek man by nature, Carl wasn't nearly as physically fit as Nathan despite being almost ten years younger. Carl kept his blonde hair trimmed close to his head to conceal that he was losing his hair.

The fourth and final investor was mysteriously absent, although he was the only one working a day job in addition to his position with the country club. The missing investor was Dr. Brian Murdock, Professor's associate at the museum.

"Oh, Jacey," Nathan announced cheerfully. "You're back from lunch. Good. If anyone is looking for us, we'll be in the Men's Smoking Lounge."

"Yes, sir."

The term 'Men's Smoking Lounge' was almost enough to make Jacey sneer with disgust. She was definitely in the middle of the boys' club. For some reason, wives of wealthy club members overlooked sexism at the country club. They seemed perfectly contented with their Garden Room parties and other snotty, froo froo frilly women stuff. Another reason Jacey felt out of place often. She was always more of a tom girl. The only thing girly about her was her work attire and the hideous purse she carried. Both things would easily fall by the wayside if she worked at the library or the press. Men's Smoking Lounge! No women allowed! She had half a mind to snag one of Asher's stogies and light up in front of all the 'men' in the Men's Smoking Lounge. Her fantasy was short lived as she watched Carl and Nathan leave the reception area.

Davis stopped at Jeannette's desk and sorted through some mail. He didn't seem in much of a hurry to join his fellow board members. Jacey knew he was seeking confidential mail. It was his usual practice to leaf through the stack of mail looking for anything marked confidential. She didn't know why he insisted on searching through the mail. Jacey and Jeannette were always diligent about placing confidential mail on their bosses' desks and never mistakenly opened those letters. Jacey had to admit, she was curious about their confidential mail. The return address was always vague. Usually just Stony Ridge, the state, and zip code. When Davis didn't find anything to his liking in the pile of mail, he approached Jacey's desk and offered his usual, pleasant smile.

"Is Asher back from his business trip yet?" Davis asked, seemingly making small talk.

"No, not for a few more days," she replied and felt herself smile more naturally.

She liked when people mentioned Asher by name in general conversation. Not so long ago, most feared breathing his name, and if they did, it was never in a good way.

"I hate when he misses poker night at the museum," Davis remarked then shook his head. "Someone needs to keep Timon in line."

Jacey laughed at the comment. She'd witnessed Timon playing poker with the boys. He was about as serious with his poker game as he was with everything else, which wasn't saying much. The reception office door opened to reveal a tall, well-built man with a pleasant but stern look about him. Nick was the man Jacey fondly referred to as 'the muscle'. He was technically in charge of security, but he did have a certain henchman appeal. Handsome by anyone's standards, Nick was a lady's man, or so Jacey had heard. He'd made his way around the female employees at the club, although none could keep his attention longer than five minutes after the dirty deed was done.

"Roxy's looking for you, sir," Nick announced without acknowledging Jacey.

As with most young, single female employees, Nick had suavely put the moves on Jacey. She politely informed him she was involved. Of course, he wasn't about to let that get in his way and stepped up his propositions. When Asher dropped by for lunch, Nick learned of her unusual friendship with the local legend and that was enough to sever all interest. Despite Asher's restored reputation, some still avoided him at any cost. Jacey had to admit, being friends with Asher did tighten her circle. Some people avoided her based solely on her association with the infamous man. Davis nodded to Nick in response. Nick left without further comment. Davis then smiled pleasantly at Jacey.

"Can't keep my daughter waiting," Davis announced cheerfully. "She's filling in as receptionist next week while Diane's on vacation."

"I heard she's very excited," Jacey replied. "We've already made plans to have lunch together."

"I appreciate that, Jacey," he announced. "It can be intimidating being the new girl. I only want my daughter to be happy."

"It wasn't that long ago when I was the new girl, so I know how she feels," she remarked then flashed a teasing smile.

Davis held back his laugh. "I sometimes forget you're technically still new," he replied. "You've only been here two months and you run circles around Jeannette."

"In Jeannette's defense, she's only been here a month longer than me," Jacey informed him. "I think she just needs to get used to working a full-time job."

"Perhaps," he replied but didn't appear interested in the subject. "I'll be back later. Hold my calls." Davis smiled and hurried from the room.

Chapter Six

The exclusive neighborhood was bustling with activity on the warm, sunny afternoon. Women pushed young children in strollers, children rode their bikes along the quiet streets, and several lawn service companies tended to the landscaping of the wealthy homes. Jeannette's house seemed quiet compared with the other homes surrounding hers. Within the large sitting room, Jeanette paced the length of the room. Despite her flawless make-up and perfect hair, she looked stressed from last night's ordeal. Her bruised cheek was almost completely hidden behind a layer of concealing make-up, but it wasn't enough to erase the bruise altogether. She picked up her glass of whiskey and drained the remaining contents. She approached the portable bar and immediately refilled her glass. She took another large swallow then hesitated and removed a flash drive from the cleavage of her shirt. She flexed her hand over the thumb drive several times before returning it down the front of her shirt. She drank the entire glass of whiskey then hurried from the sitting room and down the hall.

Jeannette crossed the massive study and flopped into the antique leather chair behind the elegant, carved desk. She snatched a padded envelope from the bottom drawer and found a pen lying on top of the desk. She was about to write on the envelope then hesitated and carefully considered her next move. She tapped the tip of the pen on the envelope a moment then carefully printed the name 'Konrad Asher' on the front. It didn't take long to find his address in her husband's old rolodex. She removed the flash drive from her cleavage and, with trembling hands, slipped it into the envelope. She then sealed the envelope and placed several stamps on it, not caring if she used too many. Jeannette jumped up from the chair and hurried from the room.

Within minutes, Jeannette was walking down the residential street toward the blue postal drop box near the entrance of the exclusive development. She placed the envelope into the drop box then stared at it for several minutes while chewing on her fingernail. Her distressed look remained. She ran trembling fingers through her hair and exhaled softly.

†

Jacey sat before her desk with the phone to her ear while scribbling notes onto the phone message pad. Two other lines were ringing simultaneously. She had set Jeannette's line to ring on her phone, so she wouldn't have to jump from desk to desk. She could barely concentrate on her caller while listening to the phone ringing on two other lines. Jacey thanked her caller, hung up the phone, and then glared at the flashing red lights. She cried out with frustration and hit the 'out of office' button. All three lines silenced. Jacey groaned softly while holding her head. The silence was a welcomed relief. She snatched a large pile of papers from the 'out' bin and left the office.

Just a short walk down the back corridor took Jacey to the basement file room. She escaped through the door and down the dingy, wooden stairs. Once within the basement, there were four rows of metal shelving containing file boxes nearly up to the ceiling. She walked past the four rows filled with boxes and escaped to the back corner. There was a large wooden bench, a small table, and an industrial sized shredder in the back corner. Several bags filled with shredded files were lined against the back shelf. The room was completely silent, being the only place Jacey knew to escape her bad days. She collapsed on the bench and lazily fed documents through the large shredder. She heard the door open at the top of the steps and listened a moment.

"Jacey?" came the familiar male voice.

Jacey drew a deep breath and was almost relieved. "Down here, Brian!"

She listened to the footfalls creaking on the old steps. A man in his late twenties appeared in the aisle in which she hid. Brian Murdock was the fourth board member and Professor's colleague at the museum. He was a sharp dressed, handsome man with short brown hair and a million dollar smile. Brian was a known womanizer but had wormed his way into her life through Maxwell and the other scientists, who were now her friends. Theirs was a complex relationship ever since the scientists took up shop at the institute a little over three months ago. He glanced over where she sat in the corner of the aisle.

"Davis said I'd probably find you here," Brian remarked and again glanced around, giving her an odd look. "Are you hiding from someone?"

"Just the relentless ringing of phones," she replied. "What brings you to my dungeon?"

"Professor said you were having a rough day, so I thought I'd drop by and see if there was anything I could do," Brian replied with sincerity.

"Can you command the phones to stop their endless ringing?" she asked with a sly grin on her face.

"No," he replied with a chuckle. "I'm afraid that's out of my hands." Brian sat on the bench near her and appeared sympathetic. "I know you're overworked with Jeannette calling out every other day, and I realize you're frustrated with a lot of the problems around this place."

"Oh?" she asked while raising her brow. "Which problems are you referring?"

"Come on, Jacey," he announced firmly while studying her. "It's me. We both know this place is the last of the boys' clubs. It's filled with sexist, egotistical men parading around their trophy wives. And when they're finished, they put them back in the china cabinet for safekeeping. Most of the women in town want to see the club members strung up by their balls. You don't have to pretend with me."

"Wow," she remarked while staring at him with a surprised look on her face. "Some pretty harsh words coming from one of the four remaining investors."

"I have big plans for this place, Jacey," he informed her. "Carl and I want to change the club into something better for everyone. If we get the right person to invest and become the fifth board member, we can get things done the right way."

"And your point?"

"Just stick it out a while longer," Brian replied, although he almost seemed to be begging. "I promise you, it'll get better. Carl and I are working on it."

Jacey stared at him while frowning. "I have little choice but to stick it out," she informed him. "I can't afford to go back to the library and the paper. I racked up my credit card buying upscale clothing for this job."

"I know it sucks," he informed her, "but I'm going to make it better. You'll be glad you decided to stay on. Just give me a month or two. You'll see."

Jacey stared at him a moment then smiled and laughed softly. "Honestly, Brian, you're the last person I would have expected to stand up for women's rights at the club."

"Are you kidding?" he suddenly proclaimed. "That shit turns women on."

She glared at him. He grinned causing her to laugh. Brian patted her arm, stood, and kissed her cheek.

"You just take it easy," he informed her. "I'll bring up Jeannette's constant absenteeism at our next meeting."

"Good luck with that," she muttered under her breath. "I'm afraid you have some strong opposition. Of course, now that you're dating Roxy--"

Brian made a face. "Yeah, that didn't exactly work out," he replied. "She sort of dumped me."

Jacey groaned softly and shook her head. "Who was it this time?"

"You'll hear about it soon enough," he replied. "If we're lucky, some racy photos might start to circulate."

She eyed him with surprise, although she shouldn't have been. "You're a dog, Brian," she muttered.

He grinned. "Woof woof."

Jacey wanted to scold him, but it would be a waste of time. "Why would you document your affairs?" she demanded while folding her arms across her chest. "What possible good could ever come from such things?"

"Hey, I'm not the one doing it," Brian insisted while attempting to look innocent. "There's some lunatic running around peeping in windows, taking dirty pictures, and demanding money."

He casually shrugged. "I have nothing to lose by those photos being leaked, so what do I care."

Jacey stared at him with surprise. "You mean someone's trying to blackmail you?"

He snorted a soft laugh. "Yeah, pretty humorous, huh? It was just that one time before I started dating Roxy. I don't know why they threatened to show those pictures, but I didn't pay and nothing happened. I'm thinking it was the girl I was with in the picture trying to get revenge or something." He flashed a smile. "I'll leave you to your, uh, filing."

She shook her head and laughed as he left. It was nice she was able to joke around with Brian these days, particularly at his womanizing ways. She was just thankful she'd never been suckered into the drama of dating him.

Chapter Seven

It was the end of an exhausting day. Jacey felt relief as she finally shut down her computer and locked her desk drawer for the evening. If she hadn't said it before, Mondays sucked. She was already exhausted and she still had an entire evening of work ahead of her. All she wanted to do was saddle her horse and go for a lengthy ride where there weren't any phones. Since she took the job at the country club, there wasn't time for that sort of thing during the week. Maybe she would be better off broke working for next to nothing at the library and the paper. Life seemed much simpler then. She walked away from the desk and toward the office door with her keys in her hand and her purse nearly dragging on the floor behind her. The phone rang, striking a raw nerve inside her. She considered not answering it, but it was still one minute until five o'clock. On the second ring, she groaned and reluctantly returned to her desk. She snatched the phone from its cradle and attempted a cheerful tone.

"Nathan's office."

"Oh, Jacey," Jeanette chirped through the phone from the other end. "I'm glad I caught you."

"Hey, Jeanette. Are you feeling--?"

"Can you stop by my place before you head home?" Jeannette suddenly asked without letting her get in a word. "I really need to talk to you. It's important."

Jacey wasn't sure, but it sounded as if Jeannette was drunk. She didn't have time to indulge the woman's need for attention or listen to drunken ramblings.

"Could I call you after I get home? I really have--"

"It's really important, Jacey," Jeannette informed her. There was a brief hesitation. "It has to do with Konrad Asher."

Jacey felt her body tense. Jeannette had said the magic words. It was difficult for Jacey to refuse anything involving Asher, especially when it came to damage control. She became Asher's self-proclaimed P.R. person the moment their friendship finally stepped out of the shadows and into the light of day. Not that Asher cared about his reputation, but Jacey certainly did.

"Well, okay. But only for a few--"

"Thanks, Jacey," Jeannette chirped. "You'll thank me for it later."

Before Jacey could even mutter a good-bye, Jeanette hung up. Jacey shook her head and just about slammed the phone down with disgust.

"Another drama queen moment," Jacey muttered. "Thanks, Jeanette."

Just one more item to add to her lengthy 'to do' list for the evening. She hoped to get to bed at a decent hour, but it wasn't looking good.

✝

Jeanette hung up the phone where she sat behind the desk in Doyle's study. She leaned back in the chair, and, despite her drunken condition, she appeared distraught and nervous. There was a thump from another room on the first floor. Jeanette quickly sat forward and listened intently. Although she didn't hear anything, she removed a letter opener from the desk drawer as a precaution. She slowly stood, attempting to maintain her balance, and approached the door with some unsteadiness. She uncertainly peered into the hall.

The hall was empty and quiet. Jeanette stepped into the hallway with the letter opener clutched in her hand. She slowly headed toward the front door while listening for any sound, although there wasn't any. As she passed the dining room while heading toward the sitting room, someone silently stepped into the hallway behind her. Jeanette slowly approached the front sitting room not far from the front door. A floorboard creaked behind her. Jeanette gasped and spun around, but to her surprise, there was no one there. She groaned but remained tense.

"Take it easy," she muttered softly and drew a deep breath. "It's just your imagination."

Jeanette lowered the letter opener and appeared to relax. The front door creaked. She looked back at the door and saw it was open slightly and moving from a gust of wind. Jeanette suddenly appeared alarmed. She turned toward the hall table phone and came face-to-face with a masked man dressed in black. Jeanette screamed, dropping the letter opener, and jumped backward. A slashing knife nearly sliced her arm. She screamed again and ran toward the partially open front door. She attempted to pull it open the rest of the way, but the man was directly behind her now with his knife ready to strike. She bolted away from the door to avoid him. He crashed into the doorframe while slashing at her at the same time. She screamed and jumped back but not soon enough. The knife scratched her upper arm. She continued to scream, unaware of her minor injury, and ran up the stairs. The intruder chased after her and remained only steps behind her.

There was the thumping of two sets of running feet up the carpeted stairs. As Jeanette reached the top of the stairs, the intruder tackled her just before the top, knocking them both to the steps. Jeanette screamed and kicked the intruder several times until he released her. She scrambled up the last few steps just as he thrust down with his knife. The knife embedded through the carpet and into the floor beneath, narrowly missing her leg. Jeanette screamed and ran along the second floor hallway. She bolted into a nearby bedroom and slammed the door behind her.

Chapter Eight

It only took Jacey five minutes to reach the exclusive neighborhood where her wealthy co-worker lived. Jacey's old, moderately worn jeep pulled up to the expensive home. She got out of her jeep, looked at her watch, and groaned softly. She hoped it would be a short visit, since her entire evening was pretty much booked. Jacey headed up the porch steps to the eerily silent home. The neighborhood was fairly quiet as well, being most of the children were called home for dinner. Jacey felt lucky she had a decent lunch with the guys, since she probably wouldn't sit down to eat until well after seven. It dawned on her that there was practically nothing to eat at either her house or Asher's. She certainly didn't intend to stop anywhere else tonight. Finding a pack of crackers would probably be the extent of her luck. She paused before the front door then noticed it was partially open.

She hesitated and stared at the door as a pang of concern swept through her. Jeannette was expecting her, and she had spoken to her only five minutes ago. Perhaps she'd left the door open for her. Still, Jacey had grown cautious over the last couple of months.

She slowly pushed the door open and peered inside as she stood in the doorway. She stared into the elegant hallway then glanced up the broad staircase.

"Jeanette?"

There was no response. Of course, if Jeannette was in the kitchen, she may not hear someone at the door. It was a big house. Perhaps she should have rang the doorbell rather than call for her. As Jacey contemplated ringing the bell from where she stood in the open doorway, she heard a clunk from upstairs. She again looked at the stairs and felt slightly apprehensive. She wasn't sure what she had heard and listened a moment while remaining frozen in the doorway. When she didn't hear anything, she uncertainly approached the staircase and paused at the bottom. She stared up to the second floor and again listened.

"Jeanette?" she called a little louder.

There was still no response. Jacey cautiously walked up the stairs while remaining alert to any unusual sounds or movement. She hated that the incident at the museum three months ago had turned her into Asher's paranoid clone. Jacey reached the top of the stairs and looked around. She saw a faint red tinging on the carpet at the top of the stairs. Without giving it a second thought, she headed down the hallway. Jacey felt uneasy walking around the woman's house, even if she was technically invited. Every bedroom door along the second floor hallway was open, allowing light to filter into the otherwise unlit hallway. Jacey glanced into each room as she passed then paused before one of the partially shut doors. The doorjamb was freshly splintered. She wanted to investigate the unusual splintering, but she felt a pang in her stomach telling her to check the room first. She pushed the door open the rest of the way and peered inside. Her eyes were immediately drawn to someone lying on the floor beyond the bed. Although she only saw a woman's bare legs, she knew it had to be Jeannette. Who else would it be?

"Jeanette!" she cried out and ran across the room toward the fallen woman.

Jacey stopped at the foot end of the bed near Jeannette's feet and stared at her co-worker on the floor. Jeannette lie in an unnatural position with blood soaking through her once white blouse. Her eyes were open and transfixed on the ceiling, the horror still clearly on her face, and her mouth opened as if she had attempted to scream but was unable. Jacey stared frozen in terror at the dead woman. The stab wounds were clearly visible beneath the tears in her blood-soaked blouse. She'd been stabbed several times and the viciousness of the attack was evident by the deep wounds. Although

Jacey only stood over the dead woman a few seconds, it felt much longer. She couldn't get over how much blood covered the woman and how fresh it looked. Her mind reeled as she contemplated screaming or convincing her body to move for the bedside phone. Her mind then screamed at her, reminding her that she'd only spoken to Jeannette five minutes ago. Five minutes? Fresh blood? Did that mean--?

Jacey slowly turned her head and looked at the nearby, walk-in closet. Her heart was pounding as she stared at the partially open closet door. She needed to call the police! She needed to get the hell out of the bedroom! Somehow, she couldn't convince her body to do either. She could hear Asher's voice screaming in her head. He was telling her to run. She stared at the partially open closet door then turned and bolted for the bedroom door. She swore she saw the closet door move behind her, but she wasn't about to stop or look back. Jacey ran from the room, thundered down the hallway as fast as her pumps would allow, and raced down the broad staircase, her shoes thumping loudly down every step. How she managed to keep from falling was a miracle. She wasn't stopping to make a phone call to the police; she wasn't looking back; she was just getting the hell out of the house. As she ran down the last few steps, she collided with a large, black blur. Before she could even scream, Jacey and the stranger were thrown to the floor together, his body nearly crushing hers.

She scrambled to her feet and got a good look at the man dressed in something resembling black combat gear and a black ninja mask. He reached for the discarded, shiny new hunting knife near his black gloved hand. Jacey kicked the knife from his reach, causing it to slide across the hardwood floor and into the study. The man jumped to his feet and faced her from only a few feet away. There was an odd, tense moment as the killer stared at her. Jacey knew she should run for the door, but despite the fear surging through her, she took a defensive fighting stance and locked eyes with the killer. She didn't move and held her fist tight, prepared to strike the moment he moved. She was wearing a skirt and one-inch heels. How she expected to defeat a killer was beyond even her. To her surprise, the killer bolted for the door. Jacey stared after him with astonishment. She ran for the door, slammed it shut, and turned the bolt. She remained motionless a moment and then finally released her breath. Jacey then darted to the hall table and grabbed the phone.

Before she could dial 911, she heard the creaking of floorboards from the second floor, indicating someone was still upstairs. Jacey stared at the ceiling and swore she heard someone in the hallway. Jacey clutched the cordless phone and ran into the nearby study. She slammed the door behind her and locked it for good measure. With a trembling hand, she called the police. As the phone rang on the other end, she glanced across the study and saw the room had been ransacked with papers and objects carelessly thrown everywhere. Doyle's expensive, gold pocket was resting on the edge of the desk undisturbed. That it had been left behind seemed odd.

✝

The McMurray farmhouse, belonging to Jacey's mother and stepfather, had been remodeled several years ago. The plantation style house had an amazing wraparound porch with hanging plants, rocking chairs, and the stereotypical porch swing near the front door. The large barn was fifty yards from the house and appeared picturesque against the setting sun. Wooden fences separated several paddocks attached to the barn and two main pastures of nearly ten acres each. Several horses grazed within the larger pastures. A black sedan was parked alongside Jacey's jeep in front of the house. It was a little after seven o'clock and Jacey had only returned home a few minutes ago. Their local sheriff had detained Jacey at Jeannette's house for nearly two hours while a crime lab came in and collected evidence. Needless to say, it was just as stressful for the country sheriff as it was for her.

Professor pulled up to the farm only a few minutes after Jacey had changed into a pair of old jeans and a tank top with a worn flannel top unbuttoned over top. Sheriff Monroe felt he should contact someone on Jacey's behalf. Since her parents were gone, Asher was away at some last minute reunion, and Maxwell was in Denver until midnight, Professor was next on the sheriff's list. Despite the horror of finding Jeannette murdered and running into the killer--literally, Jacey felt she was handling the situation fairly well, all things considered. Professor walked alongside Jacey toward the house from the barn, where he had helped her tend to a few chores. He was obviously worried about her, indicated by the way he stared with that look of sympathy on his face.

"I wish you'd reconsider and come to the museum to stay with us tonight," Professor announced. "I'm concerned about you being here alone--" He hesitated and almost feared saying the words aloud. "--after what happened to Jeanette."

Jacey collapsed on the porch step, held her head, and groaned softly. "Oh, poor Jeanette," she muttered softly then looked at Professor. "I still can't believe it. Who'd do something like that to her? Especially after what happened to her husband." Jacey's eyes suddenly widened with horror. "You don't think they're related, do you?"

"Their deaths? Related?" Professor vigorously shook his head. "No, her husband died at the hands of his mistress. That was a tragic murder suicide." He hesitated then attempted to say something comforting. "She lived in a wealthy neighborhood," Professor remarked and sat on the step near her, resting his back to the railing. "Sheriff Monroe is convinced the burglar thought no one was home, which she normally wouldn't have been at home on a Monday afternoon. She must've surprised him."

"I somehow think the coroner and homicide detective may have a different theory," she remarked gently.

Professor appeared curious and studied her. "Oh?"

She inhaled a deep, shaken breath then slowly released it. "I saw the stab wounds on her, Professor," Jacey announced softly. "Not to sound gruesome, but they were aggressive and angry. He didn't kill her because she surprised him. He was pissed. Her study was trashed, but he left behind an expensive, gold pocket watch. That doesn't sound like my idea of a burglar."

Professor stared at her a moment then fidgeted from the comment. "Please, come back to the museum with me," he now begged.

Jacey wiped the tears from her eyes, looked at Professor, and attempted a weak smile. "What did Maxwell say when you called him?"

He appeared uncomfortable, shifted, and then managed a smile. "He said to take you back to the museum and watch over you until he gets back tonight."

"I thought so much," she replied softly then smiled more naturally. "I'll be fine, really."

"Then I'll stay here with you."

Jacey stood, being unable to remain still for more than a few minutes, as if attempting to keep death from catching her. Naturally, her nerves were shot, but she felt she was handling the situation a lot braver than she thought possible. She didn't need people treating her like china. She wasn't going to break.

"Thanks, Professor," she replied warmly. "You're wonderful, but I think I'd prefer to be alone." She inhaled deeply and almost slipped into her own thoughts. She pulled herself back into reality, not wanting to let herself go. She was certain she wouldn't like what she found. "Besides, I still have to go to Asher's and take care of his jungle."

"Then I'll go with you," he insisted.

Jacey kissed him warmly on the cheek, touched his face, and smiled. "Right now, I need to be alone. I have a lot of thinking to do."

Professor stared at her a long moment. He was obviously attempting to read her and possibly decide if he should be more insistent. Apparently, he thought better of it, offered a tiny, knowing smile, and nodded.

"I understand," he finally replied. "Call me when you get back home, so I know you're okay."

Jacey couldn't help but smile at the lanky man. His concern was endearing. She was lucky to have such a wonderful, caring friend.

Chapter Nine

Jacey rode her gray horse along a well-traveled path in the quickly dimming woods. The reality of finding Jeannette murdered had finally hit her. Normally, she wouldn't take her horse out so late, especially through the woods to Asher's house, which was a thirty-minute ride at a leisurely gait. Riding her horse was relaxing, and she needed relaxing right now. Returning home in the dark would be particularly foolish, especially since there was no such thing as cell phones in her neck of the woods. There also wasn't anyone around if her horse wigged out and managed to toss her. She only had one incident where she had been thrown while riding, which involved her pony when she was a young teen. Coincidentally, it was the first time she was properly introduced to Konrad Asher, who later became her best friend. He dusted her off and helped her locate her missing pony. They were friends ever since.

The back side of Asher's secluded, modern cabin with its large, privacy fence came into view. The elaborate fence appeared out of place in the seemingly remote part of the woods, but her friend was a very private man. Jacey tied her horse to an old hitching post outside the privacy fence and entered through the gate. Not far from the hitching post was a small, stall sized shed, which was obviously designed specifically for her horse if the weather turned bad. Jacey crossed the elaborate garden and headed for the back patio and the sunroom door.

The cozy sunroom was decorated with quality wicker furniture and hanging plants along the entire length of the glass wall. There were various other plants strategically placed around the room, giving the sunroom a jungle feel. Jacey began her chore of watering the many plants within the room. Once she finished with the plants in the sunroom, Jacey entered the master bedroom down the hall and watered a hanging plant by the large window. She then shut the curtain and crossed the room to leave. She glanced at the dresser, hesitated, and approached it. She looked at the silver framed photo of Asher's deceased wife, Katie, wearing a gorgeous black evening dress. Jacey picked up the picture, studied the beautiful woman, and then smiled.

Jacey hoped that one day she'd find true love as Asher had with Katie. She often wondered if Katie knew how much she was loved. She was sure she did. When Katie was murdered ten years ago, it tore Asher apart. The town blamed him for her death and the old mental institution fire, which claimed many other lives. After the museum incident just three months ago, Asher was finally vindicated, although some in town still feared him. She hated that he secretly seemed to enjoy the fear he created. Jacey returned the picture to the dresser then turned to leave. A low creaking sound halted her departure, causing her to glance around the room.

The closet door was now partially open, catching her attention. She didn't remember it being open when she entered the room. Perhaps she was just being paranoid after the incident at Jeannette's house, but she wasn't taking any chances. Jacey stared at the door a moment longer then slowly approached it and yanked it open. A large box, which was held in place by the door, toppled from the top shelf and nearly hit her. She screamed, jumped back as it crashed to the floor, and then relaxed. She knelt before the spilled contents and replaced them to the box. Among the items was a brown, leather shoulder holster containing a government issued semiautomatic, various photos, and a bulletproof vest with the name Asher embroidered on it in bold, white lettering.

With some effort, she returned the box to the top shelf then looked at a box on the floor. She appeared puzzled and pulled it out. She normally wasn't one to pry in Asher's business, but sometimes it was the only way to learn things about his past. He tended to be somewhat secretive. There were old newspaper articles on the Stony Ridge Mental Institute fire, articles on Kate Asher's murder, and Asher's suspected involvement. Jacey studied each article. On the bottom of the box, there was a manila envelope. She uncertainly opened the envelope. There were several letters banded together addressed to Konrad Asher. The first bundle was postmarked from ten years ago. They were labeled 'death threats'. A second, smaller bundle was postmarked for the current year. It was labeled 'death threats and blackmail'.

Jacey frowned and shook her head. She removed a more recent article from a few months ago. It read, 'local legend becomes local hero'. She knew what the article said, since she was the one who wrote it. There was a picture of Konrad Asher on the front page looking arrogant just to piss off the locals. The caption read, 'Konrad Asher risked his life to save several people from a killer's murderous rampage at the museum party.' Jacey stared at the article. She heard echoing voices from the past as she drifted back to three months ago.

Three months earlier. Jacey lie motionless a moment as she gasped to catch her breath. The killer approached her. She slowly rolled onto her side and attempted to stand. He aimed the gun at her head. Jacey stared at him from where she knelt. Her eyes remained fixed on the gun he held.

"Goodbye, Jacey," he said simply.

Maxwell grabbed Jacey from behind and shielded her in his arms. The killer's finger tightened on the trigger.

"Haven't you forgotten something?" came Asher's all too familiar voice from behind him.

The killer's eyes widened. Maxwell and Jacey looked up from their huddled position on the ground. The killer spun to face the man standing behind him while aiming his gun. Konrad Asher plunged the long dagger into the killer's throat and straight through the back of his neck. The killer's eyes widened as blood flowed from his mouth. The gun fired in his hand, shooting Asher at close range. Asher was thrown backward and forcibly struck the side of the building. His eyes rolled back, and he slid down the wall.

"No!" Jacey screamed.

Present day. Jacey drew a deep, shaken breath as she slowly opened her eyes and looked back at the article. It seemed like a long time ago, yet it was only three months since that day. As she returned the article to the box, she noticed several framed photos of Katie on the bottom. Their placement in the box surprised Jacey.

Before Asher had left on his trip, Jacey was certain she'd seen the same photos on display in the formal living room and in the jungle he called a sunroom. Jacey studied the framed photos a moment longer then returned them to the box and pushed it back into the closet. She sat back on her feet and sighed. If she intended to make it home before the woods were pitch black, she'd need to leave immediately, but she didn't want to leave. Sitting on the floor in Asher's bedroom somehow comforted her. The feeling was hard to explain. She still needed to find something for dinner, and she was certain Asher's cupboards were nearly bare. Jacey finally stood while toying with what she should do next.

She looked at the neatly hanging dress shirts in the closet. She gently touched one of Asher's shirts, hesitated, and uncertainly leaned in to smell it. She could smell the faint trace of Asher's familiar aftershave. Not that he doused himself in aftershave, but it was a scent she was able to detect quite easily even from a distance. She nearly clung to his shirt, placed her nose to the collar, and shut her eyes. With Asher gone for more than four days, it felt as if she'd lost a limb. Functioning without him was difficult at times. Although, functioning with him was sometimes a challenge as well. She needed a friend right now, and it was too late to return to the museum and join Professor. She was suddenly very tired and not the least bit hungry anymore.

Chapter Ten

Jacey slept within Asher's bed beneath the covers while cuddling the extra pillow. She squirmed slightly from the nightmare she was reliving. A gunshot echoed from within her dream followed by her screams, which woke her from her sleep. Jacey gasped softly and jerked beneath the covers. She looked around with some disorientation, uncertain what had brought her out of her nightmare, and then remembered where she was. She looked at the bedside clock and groaned. It was only midnight. She attempted to relax and again nuzzled Asher's pillow, which had faint traces of the same aftershave as the shirt from the closet she chose to sleep in. The smell was comforting. She needed comforting right now.

As she felt herself slowly drift back to sleep, she swore she heard a clunk from within the house. Jacey mechanically sat up in bed while gasping softly, the alarm showing on her face. She listened a moment. It was possible it was just her imagination. She then heard the distinctive sound of a floorboard creaking within the living room. Jacey reached between the headboard and mattress and removed a revolver handgun. She quietly sprang from the bed and approached the partially open bedroom door. She stood to the side and listened a moment longer then heard someone moving within the hallway. Jacey flattened her back against the wall to the side of the door and held the gun close to her chest. Someone appeared in the darkness within the doorway and gently pushed the door open.

While her heart was pounding, she watched in horror as a man entered the bedroom. Jacey gently cocked the gun's hammer back while attempting to make as little noise as possible, but the distinctive sound echoed through the room. The man suddenly turned for her and knocked the gun from her hand, his quick reflexes startling her. Without hesitation or forethought, Jacey kicked for his groin. He blocked her kick, but she was already taking a swing and punched him in the face, dazing him. She immediately kicked for his side. To her surprise, he caught her ankle and tossed her off her feet. Jacey roughly struck the floor, but she didn't have time to consider the pain surging through her body. She saw the intruder lunge for the discarded gun, although how he saw it in the dim lighting was a mystery.

Jacey knew she couldn't let him get the gun. With her foot, she swept his legs out from under him. He crashed to the floor alongside her. As Jacey scrambled to her hands and knees, the man recovered and started getting up. There was little time to act if she wanted to get the slip on her attacker. Jacey boldly tackled him back to the floor, straddled his waist, and attempted to punch him. He caught her wrist mid swing and flipped her roughly onto her back, now positioning himself on top of her. She attempted to punch him with her free left hand. He caught her left wrist and pinned both her wrists to the floor just above her head, trapping her. Jacey breathed heavily and struggled against the man on top of her, pinning her to the floor in a compromising position.

"Jacey," came the calm, familiar voice. "What are you doing in my bedroom?"

Jacey suddenly stopped struggling and stared at the man above her in the darkness as he pinned her to the floor. It was then she realized the familiar scent was stronger than it had been from the shirt she wore.

"Asher?" she gasped softly with surprise.

An overwhelming flood of emotions shot through her entire body as her heart pounded with a mixture of relief and excitement to her best friend's presence. She wasn't sure why, but she suddenly felt like crying. Asher released her wrists, took her hands as he moved off her, and pulled her up with him while he stood. He released her hands and turned on the light. As the room brightened nearly blinding her, she stared helplessly at Asher, almost afraid to believe he was actually home. Konrad Asher was a distinguished looking man in his early forties with a slight silver to his light brown hair. What stuck out most about Asher was his hypnotic blue eyes. Far from muscular, he was built moderately athletic. Despite his build, he was stronger than most gave him credit. If anyone asked Jacey's opinion, Asher's mind was his greatest asset. He didn't seem physically intimidating, but he had an unsettling way of staring that created fear in most. Jacey never really understood it. She found his blue eyes captivating and not the least bit intimidating.

Asher casually glanced over her, raised a tiny smirk, and gently dabbed the bleeding cut on his lip. "Did anyone ever tell you, you hit like a man?"

As she stared at him now standing before her, her emotions took over. Jacey threw her arms around his neck and jumped into his arms, attempting to hold back pent up emotions from her harrowing ordeal at Jeannette's house. Asher returned the embrace, almost as if he knew it wasn't an 'I'm so glad to see you' hug.

"Oh, Asher," she gasped softly while burying her face into his shirt collar. "I'm so glad you're home."

"Yes, I noticed by the warm reception I'd received," he lightly teased.

Jacey felt her body tremble, causing her to pull away quickly before he noticed. Every emotion from her exhausting day wanted to surface, but she was determined to keep them concealed. She didn't know why she was reluctant to share her trauma with him. She stared at him a moment then covered her emotions by forcing a warm smile and kissing him quickly on the lips. She pulled back and grinned despite her urge to cry on his shoulder.

"Better?" she joked softly while stifling her sniff.

Asher chuckled and hugged her again, almost as if he wouldn't let her go. She actually hoped he wouldn't.

"Much better." Asher then pulled away and suspiciously glanced around the room. He looked back at her almost demandingly and raised a curious brow. "You wouldn't be hiding Dr. Maxwell from me, would you?"

She wasn't sure whether she wanted to laugh or cry at the comment. "No, he's not here," she playfully replied. "You know better."

Asher picked up the discarded gun then eyed her while indicating the revolver.

"Where did you find this?"

Jacey casually shrugged. "In the hidden holster strapped between your mattress and headboard."

Asher shook his head, approached the bed, and replaced the gun to its rightful hiding spot.

"You're a little too clever for your own good," he muttered while leaning over the bed.

"You weren't supposed to be home for another four days," she remarked while studying him. "What happened?"

Asher casually straightened and turned from the mussed bed then looked at her. "You found your co-worker murdered and had a run-in with her killer," he remarked matter-of-fact. "Naturally I'd be on the next plane home." He looked into her eyes as he gently placed his hand on her shoulder. His look was serious yet tender. "Are you okay?"

Jacey avoided looking at him as she slowly approached the bed and collapsed onto the edge. Somehow, she feared if she looked at him that she'd start crying.

"A few unpleasant memories suddenly came back to haunt me," she replied softly, feeling his eyes upon her.

"I know that feeling all too well."

She lifted her head and met his gaze. "I'm sorry, Asher. I shouldn't have brought it up--"

"Of course you should," he interrupted firmly. "Don't apologize." He hesitated while staring at her. "Katie died a long time ago. I've licked my wounds, and they have healed. It's you I'm worried about."

"You don't need to worry about me," she replied then offered a tiny smile. "I'm surviving just fine in denial."

Asher didn't appear humored by her joke. He joined Jacey on the edge of the bed and studied her. "I stopped by your house and then went to the museum," he informed her then appeared curious. "Why didn't you stay with Professor?"

"I thought I'd be more comfortable here."

"Apparently so," he remarked. "Even I didn't expect to find you here."

The realization that he'd caught her sleeping in his bed had then hit her. She became concerned by how it must have looked. The last thing she wanted was to disrespect Katie's memory by sleeping in her bed.

"You don't mind, do you?"

Asher chuckled softly and patted her hand. "Of course not, darling. You're welcome to anything I have," he announced almost cheerfully. "I'm just curious as to why you didn't go to the museum. Professor said you wouldn't go with him."

Jacey hesitated then reluctantly answered. "Maxwell was getting in after midnight, and I wasn't in the mood to deal with him," she replied gently.

Asher seemed surprised then curious. "Our Dr. Maxwell not treating you right?"

Although it sounded like an innocent question, Jacey knew Asher actually meant, 'if he hurt you, I'll kill him'.

"It's not like that," she quickly informed him before he could come to his own conclusions. "Actually, he asked me to marry him."

Asher stared at her a moment in silence. His expression was hard to read, but she supposed he was having a difficult time reading hers too.

"Shall I hold off on the champagne toast?"

Jacey drew a deep breath and stared at Asher. "He got a job offer in Denver."

Asher stared at her a long, uncomfortable moment. She could swear she heard his world shatter. He shifted alongside her, patted her leg, and attempted a weak smile.

"I see," he replied gently then put up a brave front. "You know I'll support whatever decision you make."

"I'm not going," she replied a little too quickly.

Asher exhaled and attempted not to smile at her response. He fidgeted slightly and avoided looking her in the eyes.

"I hope your decision isn't on my account."

"I'm not ready to move off to Denver and leave my family and friends behind," she informed him. "Besides, I've been having doubts about my relationship with Maxwell. He's just, well, been so ambitious lately. He moved to Stony Ridge to escape high society and now he's doing anything he can to return to it. He's changing into the very people I try to avoid."

Jacey looked down and appeared distant while in her own thoughts. Asher studied her a moment then squeezed her hand, returning her to reality.

"Something else?" he asked.

She feared looking at him but reluctantly met his gaze. "He could've come home early when he found out what happened tonight, but he didn't." She groaned softly and raked her fingers through her mussed hair. "I know it's unfair of me. That party was important to his career, but--"

Asher smiled gently, lifted her hand, and gently kissed it. She stared at him and wondered how he was always able to make her feel better without ever solving her problems.

"Perhaps you need to talk with Dr. Maxwell about how you feel," he informed her then raised his brow. "We men tend to have poor judgment when it comes to sensitivity."

She stared at him a moment then drew a deep breath. "You didn't seem to have any trouble flying halfway across the country to get back here."

There was an awkward silence as he stared at her. He inhaled deeply while staring into her eyes. His look was frighteningly serious.

"I lost everything I loved once," he gently informed her, which she was well aware. "Dr. Maxwell and I have a different set of *priorities*."

She understood him loud and clear. Jacey smiled warmly, clung to his arm, and rested her head on his shoulder.

"I somehow knew you'd come back," she announced softly. As she clung to his arm, she almost wished she could crawl inside him and hide forever.

"Getting damned predictable in my old age," he announced with a chuckle while patting her hand on his arm. "I'll need to work on that."

Asher patted her leg then stood, despite her attempt to keep hold of his arm. She almost wished she held on tighter, so he couldn't pull away. He turned to face her where she remained sitting on his bed.

"Why don't you get some sleep," he suggested. "You must be exhausted. We'll talk more tomorrow."

He pulled the cover back for her and patted the bed. Jacey quickly stood and smiled gently at his charm.

"It's your bed," she reminded him. "I'll sleep in the guestroom."

"Nonsense. That mattress is far too lumpy for you," he announced firmly. "Don't bother arguing with me. You know you'll never win."

Jacey had to smile then climbed under the covers and nuzzled the pillow. Asher pulled the covers up to her waist then leaned over her and kissed her gently on the cheek. He straightened and appeared humored.

"Out of a dozen clean shirts in my closet, you pick the only dirty one," he teased then laughed. "That shirt reeks of me."

She turned her head, sniffed the collar, and then looked back at him while smiling knowingly. "You're right; it does."

Asher chuckled softly. "Your sense of smell needs some fine tuning," he teased. "Good night, darling."

She watched him cross the room and turn off the light. Despite near darkness, she watched his silhouette leave the room. She didn't want him to leave. Would it have been wrong to ask him to stay and hold her while she slept? She stared at the partially open door for the longest time and pondered the answer.

Chapter Eleven

Seven o'clock the following morning, Jacey wearily padded into the kitchen still in her borrowed shirt. To her surprise, she found Asher mixing pancake batter in a large bowl. She eyed him suspiciously while running her fingers through her excessively mussed hair. He looked shower fresh and in a set of clean clothes. She was surprised he had been able to slip past her while she slept to take a shower without waking her.

"You're up early," she announced while watching him at the counter.

He glanced at her and smiled. "I could say the same about you."

"Well, some of us have a thirty minute ride ahead of us before even considering showering and changing for a full day of work."

"I'd think you'd be taking the day off," he remarked sarcastically. "Although I'm not surprised you're not."

"Can I assume your assumption has something to do with my clothes disappearing?"

"I was doing a load of laundry this morning anyway," he replied then grinned. "Yours were a little horsy smelling."

So not only had he slipped past her while she slept, showered, and dressed, he also made off with her dirty clothes. She wasn't winning any awards for being aware of her surroundings. Jacey glared at him and shook her head.

"How do you propose I ride back home?" she suddenly asked. "The woods are secluded, but I certainly can't ride in only your shirt and my underwear."

Jacey wouldn't admit it to him, but the thought of trotting her horse all the way home without wearing a bra sounded almost agonizing.

"No need to worry," he informed her. "I had a contingency plan in case you intended to go into work today." He grinned proudly. "You catch a shower and wash that Asher reek off yourself while I find something snob friendly from Katie's closet for you to wear to work. Afterwards, I'll finish making breakfast for us."

She stared at him with bewilderment or possibly disbelief. He was losing his touch or at least not thinking.

"Asher, I have to take my horse home and care for the rest of my herd," she informed him. "I can't ride in work clothes. I'll stink by the time I get to work. I have enough women looking down their noses at me already. I don't need to smell all horsy on top of that."

"You really don't give me enough credit, do you?" he asked with a soft groan. "You can take my car to work, and I'll take your smelly horse home. I'll make sure your brood doesn't starve, and then I'll take your jeep to the club and swap it for my car. What could be easier?"

She considered. "Everything," Jacey replied while folding her arms across her chest.

"I've already mixed a large bowl of batter," he announced. "Who's going to eat all these pancakes?"

Jacey couldn't deny she was starving. The last time she ate was lunch yesterday with Professor and Timon. Her stomach growled in protest.

Asher cast a glance at her abdomen and slyly raised his brow. "I rest my case."

She didn't want to argue with him, but she still wasn't convinced it was the best idea. "You're going to ride my horse back to my house, unsaddle him, and feed the other horses?"

"Why do you find that so hard to believe?" he almost demanded.

"Do you even know how to ride a horse?"

"Darling, I even know how to ride a camel," he announced while smiling deviously.

Jacey studied his grin and hid her smile. "This should be interesting," she remarked then pointed toward his bedroom. "I'll be in the shower."

"You'll find a robe in Katie's closet," he casually informed her.

✝

Jacey walked out of the bathroom in Asher's bedroom wearing one of Katie's borrowed satin robes. It was a gorgeous dark purple with a Chinese dragon on the back. Jacey was convinced Asher had bought it for his wife on one of his many covert trips abroad. As she dried her hair with a towel, she happen to glance at the bed. On the neatly made bed laid a gorgeous, casual black dress with matching undergarments. Jacey eyed the expensive dress with some apprehension then glanced at the lacy bra and matching panties. She picked up the lacy thong underwear between her fingertips and stared with disbelief.

"Seriously?" she muttered then groaned softly. "He's just messing with your mind, Jacey."

She tossed the thong underwear back onto the bed and approached Katie's dresser. She routed through several drawers, found the intimates' drawer, and rummaged through it. To her surprise, all she found were sexy undergarments. She shut the drawer and groaned with disgust.

Chapter Twelve

Jacey sat behind her desk while typing a letter on the computer. Once she finished the letter, she pressed the print button and leaned back in her chair. She couldn't help but glance at Jeanette's empty desk and frowned. Every horrible image from yesterday flooded back into her memory. Jacey sat forward and allowed her head to fall into her hands while fighting her tears. A shadow fell over her. Jacey quickly looked up being unaware someone had even entered the office. Davis stood over her with a tiny, sympathetic smile.

"You know, you could have taken the day off, Jacey," Davis gently informed her.

"I'm fine, really," she replied although her heavy sigh told a different story. "Besides, Nathan wanted these letters and memos typed."

"After you finish them, I'm sending you home," Davis announced firmly. "I'll deal with Nathan if he has a problem with it."

"Really, I want to finish the day."

Davis hesitated, drew a deep breath, and sighed. "Okay." He studied her a moment with a look of pity after what happened to her. "Roxy offered to assist you in the office. Since she was happy to help out, I agreed to it. I don't want you to be overwhelmed with typing and answering phones."

"That was nice of her to offer," Jacey replied then managed a tiny smile. "When will she be here?"

"Any minute now, actually. Just let her help you with some easy tasks to get her started," Davis informed her. "I know you have a lot of filing she could do for you. Just take it slow today." He casually leaned against her desk and attempted to change the subject to something more cheerful. "Are you going to the museum tonight to see Maxwell? Poker night, you know."

"Yeah, I'm seeing Maxwell tonight," she replied and attempted to hide her lack of enthusiasm for the subject. She knew Davis was trying. He didn't know things were awkward between her and Maxwell.

"Do you need a ride?" he offered. "I'm playing poker with the guys tonight, so I'm going there anyway."

"No, thanks," she replied with little enthusiasm. "Asher will give me a ride."

Davis seemed surprised and straightened. "I thought he was away until the weekend."

"He came home early."

"Isn't he full of surprises--"

"Apparently Sheriff Monroe called him and told him what happened yesterday," she informed Davis then sighed. "You know Asher. He was on the next flight out."

Davis snorted a soft laugh while scratching his head. "Everyone is well aware of Asher's reputation where you're concerned, Jacey. After what happened yesterday, I'm surprised he isn't camping out alongside your desk."

"Surprisingly, he hasn't even called yet, and I've been here over an hour," she remarked and smiled at her own joke. She couldn't believe how awkward it felt to smile.

Davis laughed softly and, for a moment, both forgot about yesterday's tragedy. An attractive woman in her early twenties entered the office. Roxy Lowe had wavy, black shoulder length hair, which she took time to style that morning, unlike Jacey's unkempt bun. Roxy wore high-end clothing and uncomfortable high heels that screamed 'my father is rich'. Her expensive wardrobe aside, she was a likeable young woman who never flaunted her father's wealth. She also seemed to appreciate people for who they were and not what they had. Around the country club, that sort of attitude was refreshing although unheard of. Davis approached his daughter and hugged her.

"You two have a nice, quiet day."

"Bye, Dad."

Davis left the office with a quick, final wave. Roxy stood before Jacey's desk, looked at her, and smiled weakly.

"I know this probably seems awkward to you, Jacey," Roxy announced gently, "but I had to get out of that museum my father calls a house."

"No, I'm actually glad to have the company," Jacey replied. "Sometimes the phones get on my nerves. I can't believe how quiet they are today."

"Nathan has a meeting this morning," Roxy informed her. "My father is going there now. I guess the word gets around." She suddenly seemed tense and stared at Jacey. "Is it true? Did you really, uh, you know, find Jeannette?" she asked softly then made a face. "Did you actually see her killer?"

Jacey leaned back in her chair and groaned softly. "Yeah, unfortunately, I bumped into him."

Roxy slowly sat on the edge of her desk and stared at her with wide, horror-filled eyes. "But you didn't see who it was? Not even a clue to his identity?"

"No, he wore a mask," she replied. "The typical standard height, standard build didn't offer much either."

"That must have been terrifying," she gasped softly then hesitated and shifted slightly. "Does it bother you that I'm talking about it?"

"No, of course not," Jacey replied. "Everyone has all morning. Some even to my face."

"Were you and Jeannette close?" Roxy asked then fidgeted. "I mean, that you went there after work?"

"No, not really," Jacey replied. "That's what's weird. She called me right before I left yesterday and asked me to stop by. She didn't actually say why she wanted to talk to me, although she sounded drunk. I got there five minutes later, and she was already dead."

"You're right, that is weird," Roxy remarked while studying her. "Do you think she knew she was in danger and that's why she called you?"

"Sheriff Monroe thinks it was a random break-in, and she surprised him," Jacey replied mechanically.

Roxy seemed quick to assess her look and questioned it. "You don't think so?"

Jacey sank into thought and slowly shook her head. "Too many things just doesn't add up. Nothing was missing although the study was ransacked. I get this nagging feeling killing her was the main reason behind the break-in."

"That's the journalist in you surfacing," Roxy gently informed her.

"No," she replied with a sigh and sank back in her chair. "That's years of Konrad Asher imprinting himself on my psyche." She quickly straightened and offered a smile. "Come on. I'll introduce you to the file room. You'll want to spend a lot of time down there once the phones start ringing."

Chapter Thirteen

Jacey and Roxy sat on the thick bench toward the back of the basement file room. Jacey shredded files in the large shredder, watching the many, tiny blades slice through the paper in an all-out assault. The violence of the shredder attacking the paper somehow soothed her. Her sudden fondness for violence frightened her. She had fantasized an alternate ending when she faced Jeannette's killer in the hallway. She envisioned beating the killer within an inch of his life. Sadly, the reality would probably have gone a different direction. Her skirt and pumps would have seen to it. She learned that lesson at the museum tragedy. Roxy filed papers into the portable file boxes on the small table. She looked around several times and marveled at the room. It was so quiet; it almost seemed as if they were cut off from the rest of the world; or at least the rest of the country club.

"I didn't even know this room existed," Roxy remarked then returned to her filing.

"That's its charm. No one bothers us down here," Jacey informed her. "It used to be the wine cellar. The original owners blocked off the kitchen stairs years ago before the country club even bought the place."

Their solitude was interrupted when they heard the sound of men laughing while walking down the rickety, old stairs. The stairs couldn't be seen from the fourth row of files, where they were located. Both women silenced and listened to the approaching trespassers.

"I'm telling you, Carl," Nathan announced. "You'll love having her help out around here. She's hot."

Jacey and Roxy eyed each other and appeared curious. Jacey was pretty sure they were talking about Roxy.

"Yeah, but I'll have to get past her old man first," Carl replied, indicating they were in fact talking about Roxy. "You know how protective he is over her."

"She won't tell him anything, I promise," Nathan remarked with humor in his tone. "Girls like that love defying their fathers. Give it a week. You'll see. You'll have her crawling all over you before you know it."

Roxy looked at Jacey and rolled her eyes. She motioned that it wasn't happening. Jacey held back her laugh.

"I think you're wrong," Carl remarked. "And what's in it for you? Why would you want to trade her to be my secretary and not keep her for yourself? You always have some selfish reason for everything you do."

Roxy giggled softly then covered her mouth. Both women looked at each other and attempted to remain silent. Nathan and Carl appeared around the aisle and eyed them. Both women looked up and acted innocent. Carl was immediately embarrassed by what they'd almost certainly overheard. Nathan frowned while looking annoyed.

"What are you girls doing down here?" Nathan almost demanded.

"Filing," Jacey casually replied and secretly detested him for referring to her as a girl.

"Doesn't sound like you're filing," Nathan remarked. "Much too quiet down here."

Jacey suspected, because they were *girls*, Nathan expected them to be gossiping endlessly. The fact that they were gossiping was not the point.

"Sorry," Roxy replied while grinning. "We'll make more noise next time."

Nathan and Carl turned to leave now in more of a hurry. Carl smacked Nathan on the arm as they left and cursed softly at him. Jacey and Roxy laughed at the men's expense.

"So, Carl wants to put the moves on his partner's daughter, does he?" Jacey announced while seductively raising her brows. "That didn't take long."

"Daddy won't be too happy to hear that," Roxy announced then frowned. "Of course, then he'll want me to quit. I don't think I should say anything."

"Where *would* he like you to work?" Jacey demanded, allowing her annoyance with the club to surface. "His country club is filled with sexist pigs. It can't be avoided."

Roxy frowned and sank back on the bench. "I sometimes think he just wants me to marry some rich guy and pop out babies. I'm not ready to join the other trophy wives."

"I guess he was disappointed when you dumped Brian, huh?" Jacey remarked.

"Of course," she chirped. "He had high hopes for Brian once he found out the net worth of his family." She turned on the bench to face Jacey with an offended look plastered on her face. "Can you believe he thought I should forgive Brian's affair with Angel?"

Jacey held back her surprised gasp. She couldn't believe Brian was making time with Angel, the smoking lounge bartender. She seemed a little wild even for him.

"I guess that's what wives of the super-rich do," Roxy remarked. She shook her head with disgust. "Everyone warned me about Brian, but I wouldn't listen."

"Yeah, he's pretty suave for a pig."

Both women laughed.

Roxy's look then turned serious as she stared at Jacey. "You dated him once, didn't you?"

"Not exactly," Jacey muttered. "He met an easy girl before our first date. I was spared."

"Lucky you," she scoffed. "I thought he was sincere. I never thought my first time would be with someone so sleazy. The bastard."

Jacey was surprised by the comment but refrained from showing it. "Brian was your first?"

Roxy frowned and nodded. "Sadly," she replied. "I convinced myself to take a chance on him. I mean, who was I saving myself for?"

She felt bad for Roxy and was more than a little angry with Brian. He had to have known her situation, yet he played games with her emotions regardless.

"Yours is not the only broken heart hanging from his bedpost," Jacey said with a sigh. "You're certainly not the only person in town who hates him either."

"The investment?" Roxy asked while looking up at her. "Yeah, I'd heard about that too. Fortunately, my father didn't listen to him as the others had. I hear a lot of people lost a lot of money on that deal."

"Professor and my uncle lost a nice chunk of change on that investment," Jacey informed her then shook her head. "Asher tried to warn them."

Roxy studied her a moment in disbelief then offered a tiny smile. "I can't believe you're friends with Konrad Asher," she remarked. "I'd seen him a couple of times at the museum on poker nights when Brian and I were dating. He's a member here now, isn't he?"

"Yeah," Jacey replied with a dreary sigh and leaned her head against the wall behind the bench. She smirked as she glanced at Roxy. "He suddenly felt the need to socialize himself after Maxwell got me the job here. Although it's nice Asher is getting out and scaring new people, I think he hates the thought of me working here."

Roxy stared at her a moment and appeared curious but hesitant. "What's the deal between you and Konrad Asher? I mean, is he like the protective father or the jealous boyfriend?"

"Neither. There's no *deal* between us," Jacey replied simply and found the question almost humorous. "He's been there for me since my father died. We're just very close friends."

"Oh," Roxy remarked gently then fidgeted. "It's just, well, you hear stories sometimes." Her look turned serious. "Nathan said Asher was a bad man at one time."

"Nathan's a lying pervert," Jacey scoffed, allowing her annoyance to surface. She knew she was almost as protective of Asher as he was over her. In some ways, maybe even more so. "Some people in this town still want to crucify Asher for the institute fire that killed those patients and his wife. Funny thing is the real killer was discovered just three months ago. Despite witness accounts and piles of proof, some people just refuse to let it go."

"That's right," Roxy announced seeming to recall the incident. "You wrote those articles after the museum gala. I remember reading them. I guess some people don't care about facts or logic."

"In this town, no," Jacey replied. "Asher loves to refer to this town as "Peyton Place" or the "Snake Pit". Honestly, I don't know why he didn't leave years ago."

"I'm guessing because of you," Roxy replied.

Jacey offered a tiny smile. "I actually meant before we'd met," she remarked. "He could have walked away, but he didn't. He chose to remain. Perhaps he stayed because this was Katie's hometown and in some small way, it kept her alive."

"Maybe he just wanted to spite the town," Roxy remarked and cast a look at Jacey.

Jacey considered the comment then nodded. "Actually, that does sound like Asher."

Chapter Fourteen

Jacey entered the reception office from the back hallway while leafing through a folder full of papers. She looked up and saw Nathan siting behind her desk, routing through her upper left hand drawer. He appeared startled when he saw her and attempted a smile. There was little doubt he was doing something to which she wouldn't approve.

"Jacey, I thought Davis said you were leaving early," Nathan remarked.

She eyed him suspiciously. Obviously, he had thought that. She guessed that explained why he was sitting at her desk. Jacey hated when the bosses routed through her drawers. They always made a mess and never put things back where they found them. Not that she was super organized, but it was organized chaos.

"No, I was in the copy room making copies," she informed him then tilted her head in question. "Something I can help you find?"

Nathan produced a flash drive. "Just needed one of these." He stood and appeared more pleasant than usual. "I know it's been a rough couple of days for you, Jacey. Why don't you take some time off?"

"I'd rather work," she replied simply.

She walked past him, moved behind her desk, and allowed the folder to fall onto the desktop. She casually flopped in her chair and scanned her desk for anything out of place.

"I know I don't seem the most compassionate at times, but I assure you, it's not so," Nathan informed her while watching her with more than a passing interest. He offered what was meant to be a sincere smile, but it came across somewhat sleazy. "Let me buy you a drink. We can talk and get through this tragedy together."

In her mind, he wasn't acting like a man whose lover was just murdered. He wasn't even acting like a man whose secretary was just murdered. His lack of remorse for Jeannette almost made Jacey ill.

"I don't drink, and I don't date my boss," she replied with limited patience. "We've been through this before."

Nathan looked surprised and possibly offended, although Jacey doubted it was sincere.

"I wasn't hitting on you, Jacey," he firmly insisted. "I'm just being nice. It's you who seems to think I'm after something." He seemed unusually tense after her remark and shifted. "I know you keep the company of wolves. I wouldn't dream of upsetting Asher." Nathan then offered a charming smile. "Can't we start over again? Or are you going to hold that one little incident against me for the rest of my life?"

Although she was certain that he'd think twice before backing her into a corner again, she felt it best to forget the entire incident. The last thing she needed was for Asher to hear about Nathan cornering her. Asher would do a lot more than stomp on his foot. There were times she wished she'd done more than stomped on his foot, but she was wearing high heels at the time, so it almost seemed fitting.

"Fine," she reluctantly replied then attempted to sound pleasant. "You're forgiven. I appreciate the offer, but I still don't drink."

He seemed moderately disappointed by the rejection. "How about lunch then?" he questioned. "I could have the kitchen send something over."

"I had lunch with Roxy."

Jacey thought he seemed awfully desperate to replace his dead lover with a new one. She wondered what the hell was wrong with him but held her temper. Despite Nathan being an asshole, she currently needed her job and couldn't risk offending him. Jacey reached for the discarded folder. Nathan casually sat on her desk and the folder, nearly catching her hand. She quickly pulled her hand back and glared at him.

"What about dinner tonight?" he asked while grinning.

She felt her irritation rising but attempted to keep her hostility in check.

"I'm seeing someone, Nathan," she casually remarked and raised her brow. "Have you forgotten?"

"Brian said Dr. Maxwell was moving to Denver and you weren't going with him," Nathan announced.

Jacey felt her cheeks redden as she developed a healthy dislike for Brian all over again.

"Brian has a big mouth," she muttered.

Nathan smiled charmingly and leaned closer to her. "Don't you see? You can have it all," he announced in a tone that was meant to sound seductive. "I'm a wealthy man, and I'm practically living in your backyard. There's nothing I wouldn't deny you, if you were my girl."

Jacey glared at Nathan hovering over her and the cheap grin plastered on his face. There was that 'girl' comment again. A platinum credit card landed on the desk between them with a distinctive clatter. It had the name 'Konrad Asher' embossed on it. Both looked to the front of the desk. Asher casually stared at Nathan with his hands in his pockets and a tiny, irritable smirk on his face. He looked like a cobra ready to strike and the smile only made it more chilling.

"She doesn't need your money," Asher hissed lowly with his eyes locked on Nathan. "She already has mine."

Nathan glared at Asher and attempted an uneasy smile meant to be intimidating, although it missed the mark. He stood and faced Asher, who remained standing before the desk.

"You really need to work on your personality, Asher," Nathan muttered. "Perhaps acquire a sense of humor."

An evil, twisted smile crossed Asher's face. "Well, Nathan, now you know what to get me for my birthday."

Nathan smirked and returned to his office with a sense of urgency. He obviously wanted no part of the local legend. Asher kept his eyes locked on Nathan until the door shut. He then looked back at Jacey and smiled cheerfully as if nothing had happened. It was as if it were a game to Asher.

"I think he's warming up to me."

"Yeah, I've noticed," she casually remarked and leaned forward on her desk while studying him. "What are you doing here?"

"I'm a member," he teased. "Or did you forget?"

"That would be impossible to forget," she replied. "You rub that salt in Nathan's wound every time you see him."

"Someone has her thong in a bunch," Asher casually remarked then dropped her car keys on the desk and collected his credit card. "Just upgrading that old jeep for the shiny new Audi SUV in the parking lot."

Jacey smiled and removed his car keys from her purse. She placed them in his outstretched hand. She knew better than to call him on the thong comment. She didn't have time to play Asher's mind games. He casually sat on the corner of her desk facing her and appeared curious.

"Are you riding along with me to the museum tonight?" he asked.

"Planning on getting sloppy drunk again?" she teased while leaning closer to him and searched his adorable blue eyes.

He frowned and shook his head. "One time, and you're still rubbing it in."

Jacey glared at him and raised her brow. "Once is enough," she remarked. "You're a special type of crazy when you're drunk."

"Are we rehashing?"

"May I remind you--?"

"I'm sure you will," he muttered.

"The last and only time you got drunk, you thought you were a spy for the CIA," she boldly announced.

He leaned across the desk and met her gaze with a sly grin. "I *was* a spy for the CIA."

"You disassembled the T-rex display and reassembled it outside Brian's bedroom window."

"He was being an ass," Asher muttered while straightening.

"You attached hydraulics to it and piped it roaring through his bedroom window," Jacey remarked. "You nearly gave the guy a heart attack."

"Did you miss the part where he was being an ass?"

She glared her disapproval.

Asher attempted a smile. "All right already, Professor," he scoffed. "Spare me the lecture." He then smiled deviously. "I've been a good boy. Not even a suspect in the town's most recent murder. You should be very proud."

Jacey stood, linked onto his arm while pulling him up from her desk, and led him to the reception office door. He eyed the open door then her.

"Am I leaving?"

"We're past all that, Asher," she remarked. "Don't stir up more suspicion. I really can't go through that again. You're innocent with an ironclad alibi for a change."

"If it pleases you, I'll be sure to mind my homicidal manners," he teased.

Chapter Fifteen

What was once the Stony Ridge Mental Institution consisted of the main building and the west wing, which set nestled beyond the massive stone wall and tall chain-link fencing. The main building had been converted into four floors of the new museum. Despite the outside being well-lit, the main building appeared dark. Most of the activity was centered within the lower floors of the connecting west wing. The first two floors remained well-lit in the early evening hour. Although the west wing was only partially renovated, the first and second floors had been converted into living quarters for the scientists working at the museum in the main structure. The first floor contained the game room, exercise room, banquet hall, and a formal lounge for entertaining and hobnobbing. The kitchen, laundry room, and dining room remained under construction, forcing the scientists to use the old kitchen in the main building just beyond the museum lobby.

The second floor of the west wing currently had five out of ten bedroom suites completed, allowing a room for each of the scientists. The fifth and sole female scientist in their group had already moved on shortly after the infamous museum gala, leaving one empty bedroom suite. The remaining five guestrooms were slated for construction later that fall. The third and fourth floors of the west wing were all that remained of the old mental institute, which was an attraction in itself. Locals and visitors enjoyed sneaking a peek at the old asylum, which still contained the patient rooms and nurses' station left in their original condition. More than a decade of dust and dirt had been left behind, lending a certain creepy appeal to draw in visitors.

Within the west wing's game room, six men sat around the large, professional card table and played a friendly game of poker. The game room contained two sets of sofas, overstuffed chairs, a massive entertainment bar, a large, flat screen television, and a pool table. Brian, Timon, and Professor, who all worked and lived at the museum, played cards with Asher, Davis, and Sheriff Monroe. Sheriff Monroe Carson was a stocky African-American man in his early forties. Despite entering middle age, he had a youthful, chubby baby face and a head of thick, black hair without a trace of gray. Most would mistake him for a man in his late twenties. The six men smoked cigars and played poker for little more than pocket change, indicated by the small pile of coins in the center of the table. Timon wore a necktie around his head in an attempt to keep the mood light or possibly distract attention away from his less than serious poker face. Brian anxiously fiddled with the cards in his hand while casting several glares at Davis.

"I can't believe you agreed to let Roxy work in the office, Davis," Brian remarked, clearly annoyed. "She dumped me. Do you know how awkward that's going to be?"

Davis remained more interested in his cards and didn't bother looking at Brian. "I'm not exactly happy having my only daughter working at the club either, but she wants to work and Jacey could use the help."

Professor puffed on his cigar and smirked at Brian. "Stop your pouting, Mr. Stud. You were the one making time with Angel," he remarked. "When the female population treats you like a disease, you'd better know it's your own doing."

"The game's called poker, Brian," Timon grumbled. "Shut up and pay." It was unclear what had Timon upset with his co-worker.

"I'm in," Brian muttered and tossed a dime into the small pot.

"Man, you go through women like there's a shortage," Sheriff Monroe remarked while talking through the cigar pinched in his teeth. He cast a dirty look at him. "What's wrong with you?"

"Can't keep it in his pants," Timon casually replied.

There was a round of chuckles, although the other men were undoubtedly jealous, considering none had a girlfriend to call their own, while being forced to watch Brian toss away one beautiful woman after another.

Brian wasn't amused by their mocking words. "I thought we were playing poker," he muttered with annoyance.

Davis folded with disgust, puffed on his cigar, and then eyed Brian. "If you're so concerned about Roxy being in the office," Davis remarked, "maybe you should consider begging for her forgiveness. Then she can take you back and she'll get this crazy notion of working out of her system."

Brian studied his cards and avoided looking at Davis. "Women don't take cheating on them lightly," he muttered. "She's not simply going to forgive me."

"Did you even try?" Davis remarked sternly. "You're not above groveling, you know."

Davis received looks from the other men, including Asher.

"You're kidding, right?" Professor remarked, although he possibly hadn't intended to say it aloud.

All eyes were suddenly on him, but he didn't seem to care. He shifted in his chair while glaring at Davis.

"This is your daughter," Professor reminded. "Can you honestly tell me you'd want her to take back a dog like Brian?"

"You don't understand," Davis announced with a groan. "She probably won't find a more suitable husband around here. Brain went to an Ivy League school. His family is one of the wealthiest families in the southwestern states."

He was met with odd looks from the other four men, including Brian. Asher puffed on his cigar and smirked almost to himself but withheld his comment; although it was obvious, he wanted to say something.

"You're right, Davis," Professor grumbled with disgust. "We don't understand."

Davis appeared embarrassed and concentrated on his cigar. "Can we just get back to poker?"

†

The west wing lounge was designed for entertaining and could comfortably sit thirty people on sturdy, high-end furniture. It contained its own portable bar and had large windows across the entire front wall, offering a spectacular view of the courtyard in front. If one looked just to the right though, they'd also have a fantastic view of the large cemetery. It was Doc's intention to eventually extend the stone wall along the property line, so the cemetery wouldn't be visible from the lounge. Jacey stood within the comfortable west wing lounge near the windows with her arms over her chest as she stared outside across the dimly lit grounds. She had a lot on her mind, which was clearly revealed by her harsh expression, and that she hadn't spoken in a while. Maxwell stood a few feet behind her and stared at her back. His look conveyed hostility and moderate irritation with his girlfriend. Her silence apparently had gotten the better of him, forcing him to blurt out the first thing that came to his mind.

"So you wouldn't come out here and stay with me last night, but you had no trouble staying with Asher at his cabin," Maxwell suddenly demanded.

Jacey abruptly turned and glared at Maxwell with anger and annoyance. She wanted to lash out irrationally and could no longer fight the urge.

"You weren't coming back until after midnight, so what should it matter to you where I stayed?" she snapped hotly. "And I didn't stay *with* Asher. He wasn't even supposed to be home until the weekend. It's not my fault he came home early, because he was worried about me."

Maxwell drew a deep breath and ran his fingers through his hair. He apparently wasn't ready for the confrontation or perhaps it was his own guilt for not returning early to be with her.

"I'm sorry; that didn't come out quite right," he announced gently then groaned softly. "Things will be so much better for us once we're living in Denver. We can finally put all this Stony Ridge business behind us. You'll make new friends." He offered a warm smile and took a few steps closer to her. "There'll be plenty of socials for you to meet the other wives."

She stared at him and knew she eventually had to deal with the topic of moving to Denver and Maxwell's idea of 'happily ever after'. She felt her hostility slip away, because she knew where the conversation would eventually lead.

"I'm never going to be the wife you want me to be," Jacey gently informed him.

He appeared surprised by the comment and placed his hands on her shoulders. "What are you talking about? I want you just the way you are."

"Then why are you trying to change me?" she suddenly prompted. "You want a housewife and socialite to charm your new friends. You want me to attend parties with pampered, rich women and their little lap dogs." She felt her body tense as she attempted to keep from reacting irrationally and turning their breakup into a major fight. "That's not who I am. I'm not a city girl, and I'm not into the social scene." Her look turned almost demanding. "And what about my horses? What am I supposed to do with them if I'm living in a city?"

His look was moderately sympathetic as he caressed her shoulders. "Jacey, this is a once in a lifetime opportunity," he assured her. "I'm sure we'll be able to board out a couple of your horses, but raising horses isn't exactly paying your rent. Once I take this job, you won't need to work, and you can spend more time riding, like you've always wanted."

She knew raising and training horses was barely earning enough to cover their expenses, but she enjoyed doing it. The job in Denver was *his* once in a lifetime opportunity and would successfully take away everything she enjoyed. She realized she must have been staring at him with a troublesome look, since he felt compelled to speak.

"Don't you want to marry me?" he asked with concern in his tone while desperately searching her eyes.

She felt a dull ache in her heart. The first month they were dating, everything seemed almost too perfect. She actually considered giving in to temptation and giving her virginity to Maxwell. Then he started to change. Jacey wondered if it was their relationship that pushed him to strive for something more in order to support the family he thought they'd have. The more ambitious he became about his career, the more her sexual desire faded.

"It's probably for the best," she announced softly.

Maxwell stared at her with a stunned look and let his hands fall from her shoulders. "What are you saying?"

She inhaled deeply and held her breath a moment. "I'm saying good luck with your new career, and I wish you all the best," she replied gently. "You have your dream, but I still haven't figured out what I want. Whatever it is, I don't think I'll find it in Denver."

Maxwell was almost too shocked to speak. "Am I supposed to choose between you and my career?" he suddenly demanded. "Is that what you want?"

"No," she retorted defensively. "I want you to do what's best for you. Right now, staying here is what's best for me."

Maxwell stared at her with surprise and possible hostility. "This isn't about your horses," he launched back and turned angry. "We both know what this is really about."

She suddenly raised her brows and glared at him demandingly. "Oh? And what's it really about?"

Chapter Sixteen

Within the west wing game room, the poker game was starting to heat up between the men. Asher tossed his cards down on the table with disgust and leaned back in his chair. Timon collected his winnings while gloating and chuckling, which didn't settle well with any of the men. Monroe chewed on his cigar and glared at the jovial scientist.

"No one likes a gloating winner," Monroe grumbled then became further agitated. "And take that ugly, stupid ass tie off your head!"

Timon appeared offended by the comment. "This is my good luck tie," he protested.

"Don't believe him," Professor remarked while puffing on his cigar then collected the cards. "He took it from Doc's closet. I doubt he even owns a tie."

Jacey entered the game room as Professor shuffled the cards for their next hand. She received several looks from the guys at the table as she approached Asher. She didn't pay much attention to the others. They obviously sensed something was bothering her by her fast gait but none commented. Asher collected his cards and smiled pleasantly at her as she approached him.

"Playing cards with us, darling?"

Jacey stood behind him where he sat, gently placed her hands on his shoulders, and looked at the cards he barely revealed. His mannerisms indicated he was an excellent card player. His small pile of coins told a different story.

"Just thought I'd hang out with the guys for a while," she replied softly while keeping close to him.

Asher grinned proudly and patted Jacey's hand on his shoulder. He discarded one card for an inside straight. Maxwell entered the game room with a mission in mind and quickly approached her. When he saw her leaning on Asher's shoulder, he kept his distance.

"That's hardly fair just walking out like that," Maxwell boldly announced.

Jacey didn't bother looking at him and remained calm. "There's nothing more to say."

"There certainly is," Maxwell demanded. "For starters, you can stop this childish nonsense and grow up."

"Me?" Jacey snarled and glared at him while clutching Asher's shoulders with enough vigor to catch his attention. "I've done the mature thing. I'm sorry if it wasn't what you wanted to hear, but that's not my problem."

The men continued to play poker and attempted to ignore the feuding couple. Brian appeared to be the only one listening to their conversation, although they all undoubtedly were but politely hid the fact.

Maxwell's look remained harsh as he continued to glare at her and her secured location behind Asher. "And I'm sure I know where that decision came from."

Despite holding a straight in his hand, Asher cast his cards down with disgust. "I fold," Asher grumbled.

Maxwell glared demandingly at Asher's profile. "Something you'd like to say, Asher?"

Asher didn't look up while remaining stiff and emotionless. "Nothing you'd want to hear, Maxwell," he replied dryly in a tone that unnerved the others.

Jacey was furious with Maxwell, and she wasn't holding back on her verbal assault. "Don't start with that again," she snapped and finally released Asher's shoulders. "I told you; Asher has nothing to do with my decision."

"I think it's about damned time you severed his apron strings and got out from under him," Maxwell remarked.

Asher slammed his hands on the table, causing everyone's drinks to vibrate from the force. He abruptly shot up from the table, knocking his chair to the floor, and turned toward Maxwell. It wasn't often Asher lost his temper, but when he did, nothing good would come of it. Every man at the table leaped to their feet and jumped between Maxwell and Asher. Timon grabbed Maxwell's arm and kept him from getting any closer to the town's most feared resident. Jacey stepped in front of Asher, knowing he'd never go through her, and placed her hands to his shoulders in an attempt to calm him. Asher's gaze remained frozen and fixed on Maxwell. The look in his eyes frightened her. She swore his eyes turned a darker shade of blue. Maxwell pulled away from Timon and left the room without another word. Jacey allowed her hands to fall from Asher's shoulders as she exhaled nervously and then met his gaze.

"Can we go?"

Asher calmly and casually picked up his chair then pushed it closer to the table. He looked at his poker buddies and attempted a pleasant smile.

"Sorry for disrupting the game," Asher announced casually as if nothing had happened. "We'll try again next week." He bid them goodnight, placed his hand to the small of Jacey's back, and then guided her from the room.

†

Asher's black SUV pulled up to Jacey's house not more than twenty minutes later. She'd left the porch light on for her return, although she hadn't expected to be home so early. The vapor light above the barn lit the large area surrounding the paddock and the front porch area as well. Jacey got out of Asher's car and fumbled with her house keys as she approached the porch. Asher got out of the car more slowly and followed her with his hands in his pockets. The expression on his face was difficult to read but something was obviously bothering him. Rather than unlock the door, Jacey leaned against the railing and stared at the keys in her hand. Asher sat on the railing, leaned against the support beam, and studied her a moment in silence before speaking.

"About what Dr. Maxwell said," he began then hesitated. "Do you feel that way? Do I need to cut the apron strings?"

Jacey slid down the railing, leaned against him, and rested her head on his shoulder. He immediately placed his arms around her in a warm embrace and nuzzled the top of her head with his cheek. She inhaled deeply and sighed softly.

"There was a time when I wasn't allowed to tell people you were my friend. It wasn't that long ago when no one accepted you," she announced then lifted her head and met his gaze. "I like having you around, Asher. Any man who wants to date me will just have to accept the entire package." She straightened proudly. "I know you've made an effort to stay out of my relationship with Maxwell to ensure we were given a chance, but I'm not ready to have you cut those apron strings just yet."

Asher inhaled deeply and smirked. He almost seemed pleased by the way the evening turned out. "Well, with Dr. Maxwell successfully out of the picture, I suppose that'll give us more time for Karate lessons."

Jacey eyed him suspiciously and cocked her head slightly. "Asher, are you happy that I broke up with Maxwell?"

Asher hesitated then frowned. "He asked me to back off and said some very rude things about my intentions toward you." He then considered his own comment. "I wouldn't doubt you heard similar remarks earlier from him as well. Out of respect for you, I refrained from busting his jaw," he remarked almost matter-of-fact. "You know I only want to see you happy, but I was starting to doubt it would be with Dr. Maxwell." Asher grinned almost playfully in light of her breakup. "I promise we'll find someone suitable for you."

"Don't do me any favors," she muttered then sighed. "I think I'd like to enjoy life without the pressures of dating for a while. I'd like to just spend time with you, Timon, Professor, and my horses."

Asher affectionately caressed her hand and grinned. "In that case, I'll just tighten my apron strings and work on my growl," he teased.

"Your growl doesn't need any work," she informed him then laughed. "Night, Asher."

"Good night, darling."

Asher kissed her on the cheek then gently caressed her face before leaving the porch. She approached the door and unlocked it. Jacey hesitated and then looked back. Asher casually leaned on his open car door, smiled, and appeared to be waiting. Jacey hid her smile and shook her head. Nothing was ever going to happen to her on his watch, of that she was convinced, and she pitied the man who tried to hurt her. After all they'd been through, she considered herself lucky he didn't do a nightly sweep of her house, looking under her bed and in the closets for the boogey man. She entered the house, finally allowing Asher to get into his car and drive away. Jacey hoped that one day she'd find a man she loved as much as she loved Asher. She'd gladly take someone just like him. Sadly, Asher would probably hate such a man.

Chapter Seventeen

Despite being slightly dreary outside the following day, the weather didn't deter club members from playing at least nine holes in the early afternoon. Most members chose to enjoy the indoor amenities the club had to offer, which included racket ball, the indoor pool, spa facilities, and the lounges. The controversial Men's Smoking Lounge existed in the far corner of the country club. It was an elegant room with comfortable leather sofas, overstuffed chairs, small tables, and a massive bar along the back wall. Fondly referred to as 'the boys' club', many people from town, including the men, viewed the Men's Smoking Lounge as extreme sexism. Interestingly enough, most of the club members' wives didn't seem to share that view. They'd argue that they didn't want the men in their Garden Room and that it gave each of them time away from one another. The Men's Smoking Lounge also only catered to those twenty-one and over, so only men of legal drinking age were permitted in the lounge. Being it was one of the few areas where members were allowed to smoke and drink, it remained popular among the men.

Asher stepped into the smoking room, placed his hands casually in his pockets, and looked around at the dozen or more men smoking and having an early afternoon drink. The young hostess, Lea, looked more like a sentry standing guard at her post. She seemed a little too serious for a hostess. Despite the rule of no women in the smoking lounge, Lea was the prime example of the contradiction to that rule. The young woman wore a skintight dress that barely covered her round buttocks. Her jet-black hair was pulled back into a tight bun near the back of her head with only a few stray locks falling down her face. She was a showpiece from her perfect make-up down to her stiletto high heels. Carl saw Asher, hurried across the lounge, passing Lea at her post, and greeted Asher in the doorway.

"Asher," Carl announced cheerfully. "I'm glad you could make it on such short notice."

When Carl offered his hand, Asher appeared obligated to shake it despite lacking enthusiasm.

"I had to rearrange my schedule," Asher informed him while maintaining a serious tone, "but reading my hate mail can wait another hour, I suppose."

Carl stared at him a moment as if not sure how to respond. He grinned and treated it as a joke. He guided Asher to the massive bar where an attractive yet tough looking woman poured drinks and flirted with the wealthy men. Carl gave the woman a nod, indicating Asher.

"Angel, give Mr. Asher anything he wants on the house," Carl announced.

Angel gave Asher a quick once over while smiling lustfully. "I'll be sure to do that."

Asher eyed Angel behind the bar, possibly surprised by the comment, although he hid it well. She leaned on the bar in a somewhat seductive position, being sure to flaunt her cleavage before his face, and smiled sweetly.

"What can I get for you, handsome?"

He barely acknowledged her or her impressive cleavage. "Brandy, thanks," Asher replied dryly.

Angel winked and retrieved the brandy bottle from the back shelf. Carl remained standing alongside Asher's chair, although slightly distracted by Angel's flirtatious attitude. He then looked back at Asher and composed himself.

"Brian is running a little late," Carl announced, "but I believe he discussed our business proposition with you."

"Yes, he mentioned his intent," Asher said with little emotion.

Carl's cell phone rang, causing Asher to glance at the phone he removed from his inner jacket pocket. Few people in town bothered with cell phones, since most areas couldn't get reception.

The country club and those living just outside town closer to the highway seemed able to receive a strong enough signal to warrant owning a cell phone. Carl looked at the caller ID then smiled sheepishly.

"Excuse me," he announced while indicating the phone. "I have to take this."

Carl answered his phone while walking across the smoking lounge. Angel placed Asher's drink on the bar, flashed a smile, and then tended to other patrons. Asher removed a cigar from his inner jacket pocket and lit it with a fancy, silver lighter. He leaned back in his chair and blew smoke into the air. Brian entered the lounge, saw Asher at the bar, and approached while grinning. He took the vacant seat alongside him.

"I wasn't sure you were going to show," Brian announced cheerfully. "Does this mean you're considering my offer to invest in the club?"

"It's crossed my mind."

Brian appeared curious but maintained his grin. "What brought about the change of heart?" he questioned. "I didn't think you really cared for the club."

"Revenge mostly."

"Still in a fighting mood from last night, huh?" Brian teased while hiding his grin.

"No, I don't get angry," he replied without emotion. "Revenge is less stressful and more therapeutic."

Brian stared at him, not sure how to take the comment. He then glanced at Angel behind the bar and attempted to get her attention. She glared at Brian then ignored him and walked away. Asher chuckled in his throat at the exchange.

"Another scorn lover?" Asher teased then indicated Angel. "Despite her name, an angel she's not. One day you're going to cross the wrong woman. That one is liable to put your testicles in the blender and hit puree."

Brian shifted uncomfortably in his chair as if feeling the comment. "Can we drop the subject?" he snapped then attempted to slip back into his good mood. "Carl and I are ready to propose voting you in as an investor to the other board members. You'd naturally have one fifth say in all votes, if they approve you."

"I'm not sure you're going to find Nathan keen on the idea," Asher informed him, "but if you want to waste your time, I'm open to the idea."

"Fantastic," Brian announced with enthusiasm. "Don't worry about Nathan. I think we can appeal to Davis. That will give majority to vote you in. I'll let you know when we're having our next meeting."

Jacey appeared in the smoking lounge doorway and waited for Lea to approach her.

"The front desk called and said that Asher wanted to see me," Jacey announced to the young hostess.

Lea nodded without emotion and approached Asher and Brian at the bar while Jacey obediently waited in the smoking lounge doorway. Before Lea could give him the message, Asher saw Jacey and cheerfully motioned her to the bar.

Brain glared at Asher and showed his disapproval. "Asher, men only in the smoking room."

Asher smiled at Brian and casually waved him off. "Bullshit." He more firmly motioned Jacey to him, surprising the hostess as well as Brian.

Jacey fidgeted and uncertainly approached them where they sat at the bar. She received several looks from the men within the lounge as well as Lea and Brian. Jacey immediately felt uncomfortable from the stares.

"You're early for lunch," she informed him and attempted not to look around the room at the men staring at her.

He held up his cigar and grinned. "I'm enjoying my monthly donation," Asher informed her. "Got a massage by a woman with a moustache this morning. She nearly broke my back."

"I hate to be rude, Asher, but I'm not supposed to be in here," she gently informed him and remained tense. "Was there something you needed?"

Asher's jovial mood immediately hardened, and he turned defensive. "If anyone has a problem with you being in here, they can take it up with me."

"I'll be sure to tell my bosses that as they're reaming me out," she announced.

"Just as long as we have that straight," he remarked then grinned. "Did you want to grab an early lunch? I'm prepared to clear my schedule for you."

"I can't take lunch for another half an hour," she informed him and again fidgeted at the stares she was receiving.

Asher glared at several men seated around the room. They immediately minded their own business and avoided looking at Asher. He smirked slyly and looked back at Jacey. She was uncomfortable with his non-verbal intimidation on her behalf.

"I'll meet you in the restaurant in half an hour, okay?" she gently suggested.

Asher reluctantly nodded, allowing Jacey to hurry from the room and escape stray looks from the male members. Brian flashed a smile and stood, suddenly seeming in a hurry himself.

"If you'll excuse me, I need to speak to Jacey a moment," Brian announced cheerfully.

"You're wasting your time," Asher casually replied while puffing on his cigar and watched the smoke form little rings above him. His words stopped Brian in his tracks. "She'll never go out with you, Brian."

"Our failed attempt at dating was three months ago," he protested and seemed almost insulted by the reminder. "People change."

Asher sharply eyed him. "Some for the better, others for the worse," he replied and cleverly raised his brow. "Women talk. Don't think for a moment that Roxy hasn't already shared her magical time together with you to Jacey."

Brian frowned at the comment but didn't seem interested in heeding his warning. He hurried from the room after Jacey.

Chapter Eighteen

Roxy and Davis entered the reception office after a moderately extended lunch in the fancier dining room on property. Davis joked with his daughter and gave her a warm embrace before approaching Jeannette's old desk where a stack of mail awaited. Roxy collapsed into the chair near him, eyed her father's good mood, and smiled.

"You've been in a good mood all morning," Roxy announced cheerfully. "Can I assume you had fun at your poker game last night?"

He waved her off while maintaining his grin. "Timon cleaned everyone out and gloated about it all evening," Davis replied. "Although we did nearly have a floor show. Jacey broke up with Maxwell."

"Well, everyone saw that coming," Roxy remarked.

"Apparently Maxwell didn't," Davis muttered while sorting through the mail. "He was particularly put off and tried to involve Asher in their argument."

"Not very smart for a guy with a PhD," Roxy casually replied.

"I don't know what's up with those two," Davis remarked. "They act like they want to kill each other."

"A little jealousy, if you ask me," she replied.

Davis cast a glance at her and appeared surprised. "Maxwell? Jealous of Asher?"

"No, the other way around," she remarked. "Apparently, the two stallions are fighting over the same mare."

Davis stared at her with his mouth hanging open. "Asher?" he suddenly bellowed then grinned and shook his head. "He doesn't see Jacey as a conquest. He's more like a father figure."

Roxy shrugged while smirking. "I dated Brian for two months," she announced. "You hear things."

Her father snorted a soft laugh and waved her off, returning to the stack of mail. His expression suddenly faded as he stared at an envelope in his hand. It was marked 'confidential' and contained only the city, state, and zip code as a return address. Roxy eyed her father and sat forward in her chair.

"Is something wrong?" she asked with a puzzled look.

He hesitated then looked at her and forced a smile. "No, honey, I just wasn't expecting this letter this early in the month." Davis reached into his pocket, removed his wallet, and handed her his credit card. "Why don't you go pick up that order I told you about in town? I need to get on this right away."

Roxy uncertainly stood while holding the credit card. "Oh, uh, okay."

He handed her his car keys and herded her toward the door. The door opened before she reached it. Nathan and Carl entered in a whirlwind of fury with envelopes in their hands.

"What's the meaning of this?" Nathan demanded.

"We'll talk in my office," Davis announced in a calmer tone as he escorted Roxy out the door. He then focused his attention on his daughter. "We'll talk later, honey."

Despite her protests, Davis shut the door behind her. Roxy stood outside the reception office door and stared at the frosted glass. She considered entering, but the raised voices on the other side indicated it wasn't a good time. Roxy frowned then turned and walked away.

†

After her lunch with Asher, Jacey decided to hide out in the basement file room and organize boxes for Roxy. It would give the young woman something to do after she returned from lunch with her father. Roxy was already twenty minutes late, but since her father was the boss, she doubted an extended lunch would get her into any trouble. Jacey heard the familiar creak of someone on the steps at the far end of the file room. She looked toward the end of the aisle and listened for the sound of Roxy's high heels on the hardwood floor. She didn't hear any sound.

"Roxy?"

There was no response. Jacey was certain she heard someone on the steps, and she wasn't in the mood for games after her run-in with Jeannette's killer the other day. She slowly walked to the end of the aisle and poked her head out to look toward the stairs. The lights suddenly went out and left her in complete darkness. Jacey stood motionless at the end of the aisle while feeling her heart pounding. That couldn't have been an accident. Although there was a light switch at the top of the steps as well as at the bottom, no one would simply turn out the lights in the file room without calling down first. She slowly removed her shoes, to avoid making any sound, and left them on the floor by the end of the aisle. She crept out of the aisle while keeping low and close to the shelves. She then heard someone moving around within the file room. Jacey felt her way to the wall and slid along it cautiously and quietly. She heard a clunk from another aisle, possibly someone tripping over an improperly stowed file box.

Jacey knew exactly where she was despite the darkness and darted for the nearby stairs. She reached for the light switch at the bottom of the stairs and turned on the lights. The room brightened but revealed only rows of file shelves. Jacey uncertainly took a step toward the nearby shelves to see who was sneaking around in the file room in the dark. She suddenly stopped and changed her mind. If she ran into another situation like at Jeannette's house, it could be a fatal mistake. Jacey quickly turned and ran up the stairs. She ran along the back hall, hurried into the reception office, and nearly slammed the door behind her. She hurried to her desk and grabbed a metal letter opener. Someone appeared outside the frosted reception door. Jacey snatched the phone from its cradle and was about to dial for security when she heard a clunk behind her. Jacey turned with her letter opener raised and nearly collided with Roxy. Both women screamed in response. The office door was suddenly thrown open.

Both women spun toward the door and screamed again. Asher stood in the doorway with a concerned look on his face.

"What's wrong? I heard screaming," he demanded.

Both women relaxed.

"I may have to reconsider a career change," Roxy announced while holding her chest. "This place is just too creepy."

Roxy collected her purse and attempted a smile. "I have to run to town for my father. I'll be back in an hour." She then left with a wave.

Jacey tossed the letter opener onto her desk and eyed Asher as he approached. She was still breathing heavily and held her head with a trembling hand.

"What's going on?" he asked with concern while watching her.

"Oh, nothing," she replied while attempting to control her breathing. "Just a little on edge." She eyed him suspiciously. "I thought you went home after lunch."

"I found a secluded spot out back to finish my cigar and watched the golf instructor get friendly with one of the member's wives. Who knew learning to golf involved so much bumping and grinding." Asher then glanced at her bare feet and gently tilted his head in question. "If nothing is wrong, what happened to your shoes?"

Jacey glanced at her bare feet then met Asher's stern gaze. She fidgeted slightly.

†

Jacey followed Asher across the nearly silent, brightly lit file room. He casually looked into each aisle as they passed then scanned the room while she recovered her shoes from the back aisle. When he was satisfied no one was downstairs, he joined her in the last aisle.

"Whomever turned out the lights obviously knew you were down here," he remarked. "Why else would they be sneaking around in the dark?"

"Or it could just be someone wanting to play a joke on me," she replied.

"Who'd possibly be that stupid?" Asher demanded.

Jacey shrugged and casually replied, "Brian."

Asher sank into thought, considered the comment, and then nodded in agreement. "It's possible. That boy doesn't handle rejection well."

She stared at him with surprise. "How do you know he asked me out?"

"It stands to reason with Maxwell officially out of your life, that Brian would make a clumsy attempt to take advantage of you in your *vulnerable* state."

"I'm the one who broke up with Maxell," she reminded him. "I wouldn't exactly consider myself vulnerable." She folded her arms across her chest while staring at him. "How are you able to read people so well?"

Asher shrugged. "Years working for the CIA," he replied. "Nothing gets past me." Asher then grinned teasingly. "He may have mentioned he was going to make a play for you when he saw you in the smoking lounge."

Jacey held back her laugh as she slipped into one of her shoes. They heard movement from across the room not far from the stairs. Asher immediately followed the sound without fear or hesitation. Jacey gasped and hurried after him, carrying her other shoe. She hated when he was in attack dog mode. It frightened her. Maybe he assumed he was the more frightening person in any situation. Maybe he was right. Asher walked quietly past several shelves of files, heard a sound before the first row of shelves, and then leaped into the aisle. He grabbed Carl by the shirt collar and slammed him against the shelving, causing the large metal shelves to vibrate from the hard hit. Carl cried out with surprise. It was uncertain whether he was surprised to find anyone in the file room or the fear of coming face-to-face with Asher. Jacey quickly approached with only one shoe on while struggling to slip into the other. Asher released Carl and took a step back while glaring at him. Carl held his chest while looking from Jacey to Asher then back to Jacey.

"What's going on down here?" Carl asked then saw Jacey slipping into her other shoe. He looked back at Asher and grinned cheaply. "Oh, I see. Don't worry. I won't say anything." He chuckled deviously. "You two just get back to what you were doing."

Jacey rolled her eyes and hurried past them up the stairs. Asher glared at Carl then followed her. Jacey hurried from the stairwell with Asher only a few feet behind her. She quickly turned in the hallway to face him, causing him to stop abruptly, and gave him an annoyed look. Asher appeared bewildered at the look he'd received. She pulled his jacket away from his side to reveal a black leather shoulder holster containing a semiautomatic. It was his personal weapon unlike his officially issued gun she'd found in the box in his closet. Jacey would be foolish to think Asher only owned a gun or two, but she was starting to wonder how many he had hidden around his house. She released his jacket, covering the gun, and glared at him.

"When did you start wearing your gun again?"

"When your co-worker was butchered," he casually replied. "It seemed as good a time as any to start."

"That's all this town needs," she huffed and shook her head. "You're going to get them started again."

Asher smiled pleasantly and placed his hands on her shoulders. "Don't worry about my reputation, darling. It's been tarnished for years."

Jacey didn't appear convinced but forced a weak smile anyway, patted his chest, and then sighed. "I sometimes think you enjoy your reputation a little too much."

He shrugged. "It ensures I never have to wait in line at the grocery store."

She groaned and shook her head. Once she had a chance to recover from his 'shock and awe' on Carl in the file room, she managed a smile.

"Are you sure you want Professor and Timon to come over for dinner tonight?" she asked.

"Of course. Why wouldn't I?" Asher suddenly remarked. "Unless you'd rather be alone tonight and mourn Dr. Maxwell's departure for Denver."

"No, I'm okay with that," she informed him. "I'm happy with my decision." She hesitated and grimaced at the thoughts crossing her mind. "Actually, I feel pretty good about it. Almost relieved." She glanced at him with concern. "Does that make me a bad person?"

"No, of course not," he replied simply. "It just means you've made the right decision." He then hesitated and considered the comment. "That I feel good about it, though, does make *me* a bad person."

Chapter Nineteen

Later that evening, Professor, Timon, and Jacey had joined Asher at his house for dinner. While Asher prepared dinner, the three sat in the sunroom sipping wine. Jacey shook her head while talking quietly with the two men.

"I don't know if it's Jeannette's murder or that I came face-to-face with the killer, but Asher's been acting off lately," she gently informed them.

"Define 'off'," Professor remarked with a curious stare.

"Like he's ready to start a war with anyone who looks at me funny," she replied.

"You're just noticing this now?" Timon teased while chuckling in his throat.

"He's always been, well, protective," she remarked while deep in thought. "But this goes beyond protective. I just feel like there's something going on, but he's not sharing it with me." She looked at Professor and pleaded with her eyes. "Maybe you could talk to him."

"Me?" Professor announced as his eyes widened dramatically. He reacted as if she'd asked him to walk on hot coals. "Do you think he'll open up to me?" He then threw it back at her. "You're his best friend. You talk to him."

"And say what?" she protested.

"Say, hey, Asher, are you feeling a little stressed?" Timon announced in a jovial tone as his eyes lit up. "Feel like killing anyone lately?"

"Yeah," Asher announced from the sunroom archway, "but it usually passes."

All three jumped and looked at Asher standing in the archway with a mocking smile on his face and his hands casually placed in his pockets.

"If you insist on talking about me, please speak up," he announced with little emotion. "It's tough to hear all the good details from the kitchen." Asher eyed Jacey and gave her a stern but pleasant smile. "Jacey, could I speak to you alone in the woodshed? Bring my ax."

Asher motioned her to the kitchen with his eyes. Jacey sheepishly walked past Timon and Professor. Timon watched her and jokingly dabbed his eye while pretending to sniff sadly.

"Too bad," Timon muttered to Professor loud enough so Jacey would hear. "I actually kind of liked her."

Jacey smacked Timon on the arm as she passed. Asher filed in behind her as she entered the kitchen. Asher shut the kitchen door and leaned against the frame. His look was skeptical.

"What was that all about?" he demanded.

Jacey could feel the color rise to her cheeks as she stared back at his intimidating look. "You were pretty tense today at the club," she informed him.

"With good reason," he announced boldly. "Your co-worker was stabbed to death just two days ago, and her attacker nearly killed you as well."

"He didn't nearly kill me," she insisted firmly. "I went all Asher on his ass and he took off."

Asher straightened and approached her while staring into her eyes. Her heart was pounding at his closeness. It was possibly the first time his presence made her uncomfortable, although she wasn't even sure why.

"I've earned the right to have moments of paranoia and episodes of over protectiveness," he gently informed her. His look was demanding. "I don't think I should have to remind you why either."

She firmly stood her ground and stared into his blue eyes not far from hers while maintaining a stance almost as intimidating as his. At least she thought so.

"And I'm entitled to worry about your paranoia and episodes of over protectiveness," she countered.

He groaned softly and appeared to relax. "There's no reason to worry about my mental health," Asher informed her. "I'm perfectly sound. If I were a danger to myself or others, the CIA would have retired me permanently."

Jacey didn't appreciate the joke. "A lot has changed since you retired," she informed him then indicated his home. "You've remodeled a different room in your house once a week for the last three months."

"What's wrong with that?" he suddenly demanded. "It was long overdue."

She held her breath while staring into his eyes. "For years you hadn't changed a thing. Now, you've changed everything," Jacey gently informed him then gave him a stern look. "You removed all Katie's photos."

There was an awkward silence as he stared at her. He didn't even flinch at the comment. "She's gone, Jacey," he remarked simply. "I've accepted the fact that she's not coming back. There's nothing wrong with letting go."

Jacey fidgeted while studying him. "I'm just concerned that you're having some sort of emotional breakdown."

"If I am, you'll be the first to know," he teased and grinned. He smiled affectionately, gently touched her shoulders, and moved closer to her. "My demons no longer haunt me, Jacey. You've frightened them all away."

Jacey smiled at the comment then moved into his arms, circling her arms around his waist. He held her close to him for a long embrace. She rested her head on his shoulder, inhaled his wonderful scent, and once more felt at ease, even if she probably shouldn't have.

"What would I ever do without you?" she whispered softly, although more to herself.

"Probably marry Dr. Maxwell and live happily ever after in Denver," he teased lightly as his cheek brushed past the top of her head.

Jacey pulled back just far enough to glare into his eyes. He had a unique way of ruining a moment. He caught her glare and chuckled softly at her expense.

"Just teasing, my dear."

"Everyone's entitled to one bad habit." Jacey smiled warmly and playfully kissed him on the lips then patted his chest. "You're mine, Konrad Asher."

He cocked his head with arrogance and grinned, almost pleased with the comment. His arms tightened around her waist, refusing to let her go.

"I'm a bad habit, huh?" he teased.

Jacey laughed and attempted to pull away before she got him started. He enjoyed poking fun at his bad reputation and liked it even more when she did it. Despite her effort to escape, Asher didn't release her. She did her best to avoid looking at him while keeping him at bay, bracing her hands against his chest, and avoided laughing so she wouldn't encourage him.

"You know damned well you are," she teased while playfully holding him back.

"Oh, no, you're not getting away that easily," he announced, attempting to keep a serious face while trying not to laugh as he held her. "I've been offended, and I demand an apology."

She finally met his gaze and stared into his eyes, determined to beat him at his own game. Her smile mocked him.

"You're not nearly as scary as you'd have everyone in town think you are," she announced with conviction.

Asher allowed a throaty chuckle to escape, humored by the comment. "Actually, I am," he replied. "Just not where you're concerned."

Jacey stopped fighting his attempt to hold her, stood up on her toes to increase eye contact with him, and smirked. "You don't frighten me, Konrad Asher," she teased boldly.

His grin was hard to read. Without warning, his mouth sought hers, and he kissed passionately with moderate aggression. Jacey suddenly tensed, her heart pounding roughly in her chest as his kiss sent shockwaves of desire through her entire body. It was far from the quick, playful kisses they'd shared in the past. Her hands tensed on his shoulders, but she made no effort to push him away. A thousand thoughts exploded in her mind to the wildly erotic kiss. As she felt herself giving into the passion, Asher suddenly broke off the kiss, took a quick step back, and stared at her with a shattered expression. His mouth fell open as if unable to speak. It was almost as if he suddenly realized she wasn't his beloved Katie.

"Oh, Jacey. I'm so sorry," he suddenly gasped. Asher ran his fingers through his hair with such vigor he nearly tore some out. "I don't know what I was thinking." His actions obviously startled him more than they had her.

An explosion of thoughts raced through Jacey's mind as she stared back at him, uncertain how to respond. She was certain it was true. He didn't know what he was thinking. Something was definitely going on with him, and it frightened her. Once, when he had a concussion, he had mistaken her for Katie, but this was different. She feared he was losing his mind or at least his sense of reality, which was concerning at best. Jacey fidgeted while attempting to recover from the quick but wildly passionate kiss. She felt slightly disorientated from his actions and couldn't shake the sensation of his mouth on hers. The dull ache shooting through her body was even more disturbing than his actions. With the way he stared at her, she realized she had to say something to ease his guilty conscience before he slipped into a dark place.

"It's okay, Asher," she insisted gently, although she couldn't convince herself of that. She took a step closer to him and offered a warm smile. "We were just joking around. I know you didn't mean anything by it. It's no big deal."

Asher pulled her into his arms and held her against him, obviously distraught by his own actions. She returned the embrace, needing her own reassurances. She suddenly drifted back to three months earlier on that fateful night at the museum gala.

Jacey applied pressure to Asher's shoulder wound where he lie motionless on the ground. He gasped loudly and jerked awake from his unconscious state. He looked at her with some disorientation. His eyes rolled shut.

"Katie," he gasped softly while smiling and touched her face. "I thought I'd lost you."

Jacey moved closer to him and clung to his neck. "Oh, Asher," she gasped softly. "You're going to be fine. An ambulance will be here soon." She pulled away just far enough to look into his eyes and forced a smile as tears rolled down her cheeks.

His eyes once more opened. His hand stroked her hair. "I won't ever leave you, Katie."

His mouth covered hers, and he kissed her passionately. Jacey tensed with surprise then returned the warm, passionate kiss. Asher's arm slipped from her shoulder, and he fell motionless. Jacey's mouth opened with horror as the tears flowed.

"Asher?" she gasped.

Jacey drifted back to reality within Asher's kitchen. She clung to him and again inhaled his wonderful aftershave. If he had once again mistaken her for Katie, could it be he was under too much stress? She loved Asher too much to want to believe he was hurting emotionally. Perhaps there was something more she could be doing to make his life less complicated. Or was she the reason his life was complicated to begin with? She had to convince herself that his life was better with her in it. He needed her as much as she needed him. Whatever he was going through, she'd find a way to help him through it. He slowly pulled away and sheepishly met her gaze, a distraught look in his eyes.

"You're not mad, are you?" he gently asked.

She smiled warmly and gently touched his face. "No, of course not." Jacey playfully patted his chest, despite her concerns and stared into his eyes. "We've both been under a lot of stress the last few days." As her eyes searched his, she realized that the kiss itself didn't actually bother her in the least. It was only what caused his confliction that concerned her. "You're my best friend," she insisted with conviction and again touched his face. "If you need to blow off some steam and that's how you choose to do it, I certainly wouldn't deny you that."

He attempted a smile but still didn't appear convinced. Asher pulled her into his arms and held her for a long embrace then spoke softly in her ear.

"At least you have a sense of humor about it," he replied gently.

Jacey felt her entire body tingle to the sensation of his breath in her ear. It alarmed her slightly, having never felt that before. She was reluctant to let him go. He slowly pulled away and mocked her with his grin.

"But perhaps my time would be better spent blowing off steam in the club gym," he remarked teasingly.

Chapter Twenty

Professor's sedan pulled up to the west wing living quarters a little after eight o'clock that evening and parked near the door. The west wing remained well-lit outside as well as several lights on inside. Timon and Professor got out of the car and approached the entrance. Neither man had spoken on the short drive home, although both clearly had something on their minds. As they neared the door, Timon felt compelled to speak.

"Asher *was* acting strange tonight," Timon informed his friend.

"Don't start that again," Professor groaned softly while flipping through his keys for the door key. "Comments like that only cause problems in this town."

"No, I mean it," Timon insisted then appeared concerned as he fidgeted while eyeing Professor alongside him. "I think he knows I want to ask Jacey out."

Professor stopped by the door, nearly dropped his keys, and stared at Timon with surprise. His look then turned stern and almost demanding.

"You're *not* asking Jacey out," Professor insisted with a tone of conviction then hesitated. "I'm asking her out."

"Bullshit!" Timon suddenly proclaimed with annoyance. "You're too serious for her. She needs someone fun and lighthearted."

"I'm fun. I'm lighthearted."

"In what world?" Timon demanded while opening the door before Professor had a chance to unlock it.

Professor appeared surprised while looking at his keys then watched Timon enter the building. He groaned softly and shook his head.

"Doesn't anyone lock the door anymore?" he muttered his annoyance.

Professor followed Timon into the building then shut and locked the door behind him. Both men walked across the lounge and headed toward the back hallway.

"Besides, Asher would never allow you to date Jacey," Professor insisted.

Timon glared at him and appeared offended. "Asher likes me more than he likes you."

"Not when it comes to dating Jacey, he doesn't."

"You don't know what you're talking about," Timon muttered.

"Keep dreaming," Professor scoffed.

Timon turned toward the nearby museum doorway. "I need something to eat."

"You finished that entire spread Asher put out," Professor remarked while staring at him. "How can you possibly still be hungry?"

"Don't know," Timon remarked. "I just am."

"When you have nightmares tonight, don't wake me," Professor announced then headed into the back hallway of the west wing toward the stairs.

Timon entered the lobby and walked across the large area toward the kitchen near the back of the museum. The lobby was over two stories of open exhibit space. Beyond the front desk, there was a large t-rex skeleton towering up to the cathedral ceiling. With the few lights always on for security purposes, shadows were cast from the t-rex skeleton, creating eerie shadows along the floor and wall. As Timon headed for the kitchen, he heard a faint clunk. He hesitated and looked around the dimly lit lobby exhibit. The lobby appeared to be empty except for him and the t-rex skeleton.

"Brian? That you?"

There was no response. Timon uncertainly walked back past the front desk to locate the sound. He then saw something move in the shadows. Timon appeared confused then grinned.

"Okay, who's the joker tonight?" Timon teased. "You guys aren't good enough to get me at my own game."

Timon took a few steps toward the large t-rex skeleton then stopped and studied it. He attempted a smile but the concern on his face was evident.

"Come on, guys," he whined. "This isn't funny. Come on out."

Nothing moved. Timon looked across the lobby then smirked and headed toward the front desk and the light control panel on the console. He bent over the desk and reached behind for the lights.

✝

Brian sat at the large bar in the empty, quiet game room with a drink before him and the cordless phone to his ear. He appeared annoyed with his caller.

"Will you stop worrying? I can handle Konrad Asher. He's like the family pet around here," Brian remarked and leaned back in his chair while playing with his drink. "I'm telling you, I have everything under control. Asher is not going to be a problem." Brian hesitated while listening to the person on the other end. He groaned softly. "I'm not going to ruin our plans by pursuing Jacey, so just relax." He hesitated and frowned. "Besides, she already turned me down flat--again." He snorted a soft laugh then took a swallow of his drink. "Turns out even Maxwell couldn't get her into bed." He then muttered, "I swear the girl has a gold-plated chastity belt and Asher guards the key." He suddenly laughed at the comment from the other end. "You've got that right." Brian then listened to sounds coming from the west wing. "Hey, I have to go. Timon must be home. He owes me money, and I have to get him to pay up before he crawls into his cave for his nightly bad movie marathon."

Brian disconnected the cordless phone, set it on the bar, and hurried from the game room. He entered the lounge and looked around, but there was no one there. He considered his next move, grinned, and then headed for the museum lobby. Timon was a genius, but he was a predictable genius. He'd be in the kitchen preparing his nightly movie snack. Brian crossed the massive, dimly lit lobby for the kitchen. Someone moved in the shadows not far from him. Brian saw something move out of the corner of his eye. He then paused and looked around. There was no one there.

"Timon?" Brian turned stern and again eyed the dimly lit lobby. "You better not be screwing around. You scare me again, and I'm going to kick the crap out of you. Seriously! I mean it this time."

There was no response and nothing moved. Brian frowned and continued toward the kitchen. He heard a clunk, which possibly came from the t-rex exhibit. He turned toward the nearby exhibit and studied the towering replica. In the dim lighting, it was a frightening image. He frowned with disapproval.

"Nothing worse than a scientist with a sense of humor," he muttered then called out, "Give it up, Timon. I'm not in the mood." Brian took two steps toward the large exhibit. "I'm going to do a lot more than kick your ass." He looked around the dark exhibit, hid his fear, and turned angry. "And where's the fifty bucks you owe me?"

An intruder dressed completely in black stepped out from the darkness of the exhibit before Brian. Brian jumped with surprise then groaned.

"Damn it, don't--"

An antique dagger stabbed Brian in the throat. He gasped, jumped back while clutching his bleeding neck, and stumbled backwards. The intruder remained cloaked in the shadows and watched as Brian collapsed to the floor. His attacker disappeared back into the display as Brian's blood rapidly spilled onto the floor around him. Brian gasped several times before finally taking his last breath, becoming motionless.

Only a few moments had passed before Professor entered the lobby from the west wing and headed toward the kitchen. He suddenly stopped when he saw Brian lying just beneath the dinosaur exhibit with a large amount of blood surrounding him. Professor gasped with alarm and instinctively took two steps closer, almost as if not believing what he saw. When he realized Brian was dead and it clearly wasn't an accident, he ran for the lobby desk and grabbed the phone. He saw someone move in the darkness behind the desk. Professor cried out and leaped backward to avoid the man in the darkness. Timon slowly pulled himself to his feet with the use of the desk. He held the back of his head and was barely able to stand on his own.

"What the hell was that?" Timon suddenly demanded.

Professor hurried to him and turned on the interior lights by the main console. The entire lobby flooded with light.

"Timon, what happened?"

He groaned softly while clutching the back of his head. "Someone hit me from behind." He then looked at Professor with concern. "Were we robed?"

"I don't think so," Professor announced gently then hesitated. "I think they were looking for Brian."

Timon appeared confused then looked across the museum to where Brian lie near the t-rex skeleton. Timon stared at his dead co-worker with horror.

Chapter Twenty-one

Timon sat at the bar in the game room. He held a drink in one hand and a bag of ice to his head in the other. Professor and Jacey sat on either side of him and watched him with shared looks of concern.

"I don't think you should be drinking, Timon," Professor announced gently. "Let's take you to the hospital and get your head examined."

"I'm not going to the hospital," he grumbled, hostility in his voice. "I'm not the one in a body bag."

"Please, Timon," Jacey announced and pleaded with him. "Listen to Professor."

"Leave me alone!"

There wasn't much else they could do. Jacey knew how Timon must have been feeling. She'd lived a similar nightmare. It was possible he was feeling guilty that he couldn't prevent Brian's murder. Sheriff Monroe entered the game room with a defeated look on his face and approached them at the bar.

"Are you guys okay?" Sheriff Monroe asked gently.

"What's with you people?" Timon suddenly demanded with hostility while spinning on his bar chair. The look in his eyes no longer resembled the jovial man they all knew and loved. He was hurting and he was drunk. "A man's dead! Of course, we're okay! The world's just fucking fantastic!"

Timon snatched his drink from the bar, nearly fell to the floor as he abruptly stood, and staggered from the room.

Professor groaned softly and rubbed his eyes. "I've never seen this side of him," he remarked. "I wish Doc were here. He'd know what to do."

"He's lost a friend," Monroe remarked. "Everyone deals with traumatic events differently. Considering it's only been three months since the museum incident, he has every right to react this way."

"It seems like yesterday," Jacey muttered and leaned on the bar. "It's the never-ending horror story."

There was a brief moment while all three seemed to sink into that night three months ago. Professor and Sheriff Monroe had arrived late on the scene, but Jacey and Timon had front row seats to the killer's murderous rampage. Sheriff Monroe was the first to return to reality. He inhaled deeply and concentrated on his duties regarding the latest murder in their sleepy town.

"The popular opinion poll seems to indicate a connection between the two murders," Monroe informed them. "Two people from the same office murdered within days of each other is a little too coincidental. I already know what the homicide detective is going to say about this one." He sighed deeply and joined them at the bar. "Between the coroner and the homicide detective, they believe Jeannette knew her killer, which leads me to believe this was the same guy."

"But what's the connection between Jeannette and Brian?" Professor questioned as he poured himself a glass of bourbon. "Jeanette wasn't Brian's secretary. They never even dated. If he'd slept with her, he would have bragged about it at some point. He didn't exactly keep his sexual conquests a secret."

"Jeanette and Brian didn't interact that much," Jacey added simply. "They certainly weren't friends. She didn't really care for him, and they only spoke in passing."

"But they have other common links between them," Monroe informed them. "The board members, for example. Jeannette's husband was an investor and a board member since the country club was founded."

"Except her husband died around the time Brian moved to town. They never even met," Jacey informed him. "They didn't even have that in common."

"What about the bosses?" Sheriff Monroe asked and appeared curious. "Brian was a board member, so he was chummy with her two bosses, Davis and Nathan. Jeannette obviously had a working relationship with both of them. They link her to Brian."

"There had been a rumor going around that Jeanette and Nathan had a thing," Jacey replied, feeling awkward for sharing that with the sheriff. "Some speculate they were having an affair even before her husband's death, back when she was one of the elite country club wives." She then considered. "Some believe she got the secretarial job to be close to Nathan. Lord knows she didn't need to work. She was well provided for after her husband's death. She certainly had no formal secretarial training either. She was an awful secretary, so someone was keeping her employed."

"We'll be checking into the board members and other club employees who might possibly connect the two." Monroe fell silent and studied Jacey a moment. He appeared slightly tense. "I hate to even ask--"

Jacey sharply glared at him. "Oh, no. You're not going to question Asher," she suddenly launched with hostility. "He didn't even know Jeanette, and he was probably the only person in the entire town who *didn't* harbor bad feelings toward Brian. Even you had reason to hate Brian over that bad investment."

"You're getting as bad as Asher," Monroe remarked under his breath. "I actually just wanted to ask you to get me a list of some people at the club who connect Brian to Jeannette."

Jacey felt slightly embarrassed from her assumption and outburst. "Oh, well, that's a switch."

"You know I never believed Asher killed anyone," Monroe insisted.

"Well, let's not go that far," Professor muttered while sipping his drink.

Both sharply eyed Professor. He appeared surprised that they had actually heard the comment. Sheriff Monroe looked back at Jacey.

"Can you keep me up-to-date on gossip around that place?" Monroe questioned. "I know I can trust information from you. There's bound to be some talk among the remaining three investors, and bosses tend to talk more freely around their secretaries. They forget they're there."

Before Jacey could respond, they heard a gruff voice from the game room doorway. "She'll do nothing of the kind!"

All three looked at Asher within the game room doorway. He approached them while wearing a harsh expression on his nearly cold face as he glared at Sheriff Monroe.

"I won't allow you to endanger Jacey," Asher announced sternly. "She's not a spy."

"Konrad--" Monroe began.

"Don't Konrad me," Asher snarled while keeping his eyes locked on his friend. "Jacey and I were both nearly killed a few months ago because of police fuck-ups. That's not happening again. I won't allow it."

Jacey was slightly surprised by his burst of rage, especially considering Brian had been murdered. She calmly stood and approached Asher, meeting him halfway across the room. Just by looking at him, she could tell he was agitated and more aggressive than she'd ever seen him.

"Brian's dead, Asher," she announced gently but with an agenda. "If I can help find his killer, I will."

"I don't want you getting involved," Asher growled.

His comment set her back, startling her. "What's wrong with you?" she suddenly demanded with disbelief. "Brian was a friend. You're taking this protective act to an unhealthy level." She felt her temper suddenly rising to meet his. "And where do you get off ordering me around?"

Asher appeared surprised by her tone, but not nearly as surprised as Professor and Sheriff Monroe. Asher's disbelief was quickly replaced with hostility.

"I'm trying to keep you out of a casket," Asher launched back. "Listen to me; you'll live longer."

"If I listen to you, you'd have me locked in a cabinet and only brought out on special occasions," she launched back.

Both Monroe and Professor slowly turned toward the bar, huddled over it, and pretended they weren't in the room. It was a verbal debate neither wanted to be drawn into.

Asher was visibly offended by the comment. "Then you *do* think I need to severe the apron strings," he demanded.

Jacey was suddenly feeling cornered by the entire heated argument. She didn't want to fight with Asher, but she knew something was wrong.

"That's not what I'm saying, Asher," she announced with annoyance while folding her arms across her chest. "Saving me won't bring back Katie."

Professor and Monroe looked across the room with their mouths hanging open to the comment. If they could have sank any lower in their seats, they would have. Asher stared at Jacey with a fixed glare. The comment had escalated his irritation and he wasn't holding back.

"This has nothing to do with Katie, and stop trying to probe into my psyche," Asher snapped back at her and suddenly lost his temper. "I've lost everything that ever mattered to me once, and I don't intend to go through that again!"

Asher had never raised his voice to her in all the years she'd known him, so his shouting at her was slightly unnerving. Despite his aggressiveness, Jacey wasn't about to back down.

"You already have me dead and buried," she shouted back. "Stop it, Asher. Just stop it!" Jacey glared at him with annoyance. "This isn't about me, or you, or Katie. It's about Brian, and he's dead. You can either help with Monroe's investigation or stay out of the way, but I'm going to do whatever I can to help find his killer. I'd think you of all people would get that. It's my decision to make, and you have no say in it!"

Asher and Jacey stared at each other in silence for a long uncomfortable moment. The exchange was almost frightening. Professor and Sheriff Monroe now stared at the two with concerned looks.

"Fine. I'll stay out of your life," Asher lashed out. "You'd be better off without me anyway."

Jacey appeared surprised by his remark. Asher turned and charged from the room like a raging bull. She was momentarily stunned by what had just happened and almost immediately regretted letting him leave angry. She attempted to go after him but Professor and Monroe cut off her path. It was unclear how they got in front of her so quickly.

"No, no, no," Professor announced while gently placing his hands on her shoulders to keep her from following. "That's not a good idea. Let him cool off."

"I've seen that side of him before," Monroe insisted. "He needs to sort this out on his own."

"Good advice," Professor announced.

"He'd never hurt me."

"I thought the same thing after Kate's death," Monroe announced. "He didn't talk to me for years. Let's not risk his wrath, okay?"

Jacey relaxed slightly and felt Professor's grip on her shoulders lighten.

"What's gotten into him anyway?" Monroe asked while shaking his head. "I mean, he was always protective, but that was frightening."

"I think he's either feeling depressed about Katie, or he's having a nervous breakdown," she replied gently. "He hasn't been himself for a few months."

Professor suddenly appeared curious. "You mean, since you started dating Maxwell?"

Jacey looked at Professor with some surprise. "It has nothing to do with me dating Maxwell. Besides, if it had, he'd be back to his usual self by now. Maxwell is out of the picture."

"Great," Monroe muttered while scratching his head. "That's all I need is for Asher to go psycho during a string of murders." He groaned softly and shook his head. "People still aren't convinced he wasn't involved with his wife's death. This is my fault. I never should have called him after your run-in with Jeannette's killer. I should have known he'd go insane."

Jacey was feeling the same way. She didn't understand why Sheriff Monroe felt the need to call Asher about the incident, although, at the time, she was glad he did. Now she was wishing Asher had remained conveniently out-of-state and as far from the murders as possible.

"I'll help him through it," Jacey remarked gently. "Let me worry about Asher."

"He's all yours," Monroe muttered. "Just keep him on his leash."

Chapter Twenty-two

The Garden Room was nearly empty the following day for late morning tea. Within an hour, the lunch crowd would start to arrive. Rich old ladies sat dignified at their round, white tables while sipping tea and eating biscotti. Several groups of ladies stared at one table in particular and whispered to one another. Asher sat at the table not far from them with a half-empty pitcher of Mimosa before him as well as a plateful of miniature muffins. The women watched and gossiped as he tossed a mini-muffin in the air and caught it in his mouth. The women stared with repulsion. He downed an entire champagne flute of Mimosa before removing his cigar from his jacket and lighting it. The old women gasped with horror. The young male server approached his table.

"Sir, there's no smoking allowed--"

Asher glared at the young man. He immediately fell silent and backed away from the intimidating man at the table. One of the older women huffed, stood from her table, and approached Asher where he sat.

"Excuse me," the old woman abruptly announced and glared at the cigar in his hand. "Either you put out that cigar, or I'm calling security!"

Asher eyed the elderly woman.

†

Twenty minutes later. Asher sat at a table full of older women with a grin on his face. The old women laughed uncontrollably while the two women closest to him clung to his arm on either side and nearly fell off their chairs. Asher poured the women another round of Mimosas. The waiter busily cleared away several empty pitchers. One of the old ladies on the opposite side of the table puffed on Asher's cigar and appeared to be in her glory. It was obvious all the older women were drunk on Mimosas.

"Honestly, you'd think a prince would know better," Asher informed the women as they continued to laugh. "So he gets back on his horse, determined to impress the ravishing princess, and gives the horse a swift kick, you know, to make it rear up or some manly shit."

"He didn't," one older woman gasped and covered her mouth as she laughed.

"The horse reared up, and the prince toppled off the back," Asher continued, "right into a pile of horse manure."

The women squealed with delight and burst into another round of laughter.

"Nothing impresses a young lady more than a man wearing a white polo outfit covered in manure stains," he announced cheerfully while holding back his chuckle.

"I want to hear the story about the sheik and the belly dancer again," one of the women cried out in a drunken tone.

"Yes, tell that one again," another woman announced and took a large swallow of Mimosa. "I want to hear about the dance of the seven veils."

One of the older women stood and hummed loudly while seductively stripping off her jacket then slung it around her body. The other women roared with laughter. Asher chuckled and shook his head.

"I'm beginning to wonder if I'm a bad influence on young ladies," he remarked.

"He called us young ladies," another woman cried out while laughing. "He's such a doll!"

†

Jacey glanced into the smoking lounge while looking for Asher. The lounge wouldn't be open for another hour, and as she suspected, the room was empty. She cursed softly and headed along the hallway toward the Garden Room. Loud laughter was heard, which didn't sound anything like the typical morning for snob central. Jacey entered the Garden Room and looked around. There were at least four tables of drunken, elderly women laughing and having a better time than they'd probably had in their entire, boring lives. Jacey didn't see any sign of Asher, but she had to watch the women a moment longer. One of them puffed on a cigar. She had to wonder what had gotten into the old women. She finally turned and left the Garden Room.

†

Asher stood under the spray of hot water within the spa shower room. Although there were private shower stalls toward the back, he took advantage of the closer, semi-private ones. He kept his eyes closed as the water ran over his head, along his face, and down his naked body. It was possible he was hungover, but still being drunk seemed more likely. He finally shut off the shower, crossed the shower area to the neatly stacked pink towels on the towel rack, and began drying his hair and face. He groaned softly, finally opening his eyes, and looked across the shower room at three middle-aged women clutching pink towels around their naked bodies while staring at him panic-stricken and whispering to one another. He glanced at the pink towel in his hand, again looked at the three women huddled together in the corner, and then shrugged. He wrapped the towel around his waist, stumbled toward the shower room door, and offered the women a charming smile as he passed them.

"Ladies--"

†

Jacey walked along the hallway not far from the spa area.

She stopped at the front desk and the young man, who appeared bored while sitting behind it.

"Good afternoon," Jacey announced. "I'm looking for my friend. Early forties. Brown hair with a little gray on the sides."

The young man shook his head. "Sorry, ma'am, we haven't had any men use the spa today."

She frowned and leaned on the desk, running her fingers through her hair. In the distance behind her, Asher, with his pink towel wrapped around his waist, left the women's locker room and stumbled down the hall in his bare feet. Neither saw him leave. Jacey straightened and smiled at the man.

"Thank you for your time."

Chapter Twenty-three

It was a little after seven o'clock that evening. Asher, changed back into his clothing from the night before, sat at the bar in the smoking lounge. He played with his nearly empty glass of brandy while Angel seductively leaned on the bar across from him and proudly displayed her cleavage, attempting to catch his attention. He didn't seem to be playing her game or perhaps he was too drunk to notice.

"Another drink, hon?"

Asher drained the remaining contents of his glass and pushed it toward her without comment. She refilled the glass and once again leaned on the bar.

"You look like a man who needs an understanding friend," Angel announced warmly while glancing over him in a seductive manner.

"I'm beyond help," he muttered without even looking at her and sipped his drink.

Angel leaned closer to Asher from across the bar and smiled lustfully while caressing his hand that rested on the bar. "You're not beyond my kind of help."

Asher glanced at her with a slightly surprised look. It was evident he was drunk despite his attempt to maintain a sober appearance. He seemed at a loss for a response to Angel's verbal advance. Jacey appeared in the smoking room doorway and scanned the room for signs of her missing friend. Lea approached her and attempted to remain pleasant.

"Who are you looking for, Jacey?" Lea asked in her typical snobby tone.

Jacey saw Asher at the bar with Angel, who was now turning up the charm while caressing his hand. Despite being relieved to have located her missing friend, she didn't like Angel putting the moves on Asher, especially if he was drunk, which she was almost positive he was. Jacey brushed past Lea without regards to the rules and approached the bar. Nathan jumped up from his corner table and met Jacey halfway, stopping her from reaching the bar and her drunken friend.

"Jacey, you know the rules," Nathan announced firmly in a soft, low tone as if it were some sort of secret. "Women are not allowed in the Men's Smoking Lounge."

She gave him a glaring, sweeping glance that would frighten most men. "I'm not interested in a stupid, chauvinistic rule right now, Nathan," Jacey scoffed lowly. "I need to speak to Asher. Just stay out of my way."

Nathan appeared stunned by her tone and comment. Jacey pushed past him, in no mood to await his response, approached Asher at the bar, and sat on the chair alongside him. Angel gave her an odd look, pulled her hand back from Asher's hand, and slowly straightened. Jacey studied him where he sat slouched over the bar with his drink.

"Asher, I've been looking for you since you left the museum last night," Jacey announced with concern for his disappearance. "Where have you been?"

"Drunk." Asher glanced at her, frowned while playing with his drink, and then looked away. "I really screwed up this time, didn't I?" he muttered softly.

She stared at his profile a moment and struggled for a response. She drew a deep, shaken breath and exhaled softly. "I think we both said a few harsh things last night," she gently informed him and placed her hand on his lower arm, causing him to look at her. "We're both under a lot of stress right now, but you have to be on your best behavior after what's happened." Jacey hesitated and gave him a knowing look. "You know how this town can be."

"Best behavior has never been my strong point, but I'll make the effort," he replied gently then stared into her eyes with regret. "I didn't mean to be a prick last night, darling. I can't always help myself."

"You're not a prick," she insisted gently.

"You're being polite," he replied then straightened. "In my defense, I did stop by your office earlier to apologize, but Davis said you'd called off."

"Yes, because I couldn't find you anywhere, and I was worried something had happened," she remarked then inhaled deeply and tugged on his arm. "Come on, I'll drive you home while you can still walk."

Angel approached them from the other side of the bar. She had a look of disappointment on her face then smiled seductively at Asher.

"I could give you a ride home, honey, if you'd like to stay longer," Angel announced sweetly.

Jacey suddenly felt the need to claw out Angel's eyes. Is this what awaited men in the restricted smoking lounge? A slutty opportunist willing to jump on drunken men with thick pocketbooks? Before Jacey could lash out at the woman, Asher chuckled softly, breaking the silence.

"Honestly, Angel," he announced while grinning, "I'm not that drunk."

Angel appeared disappointed and possibly offended by the comment. She tended to other members, leaving Jacey alone with Asher. Nathan approached the bar with Nick trailing behind, giving the appearance of a guard dog. Asher was about to stand when he saw them approach. He returned to his seat and casually sipped his drink, no longer in a hurry to leave.

"Here comes that prick boss of yours," Asher remarked to Jacey without looking at her.

Jacey glanced across the room, groaned softly, and looked back at him. "Let me handle this, Asher."

"Be my guest," he muttered into his brandy glass.

Nathan stopped before Jacey with a stern look on his face. "If you want to keep your job, Jacey, I suggest you leave the smoking lounge immediately. You know the rules."

Jacey stood from her chair and faced Nathan. She had to hold her temper to keep from telling him what she was really thinking.

"I'm off the clock," she announced firmly. "And we were just leaving."

"You can wait for Asher outside," Nathan informed her then proudly straightened. "He and I need to have a little talk. He'll be along shortly."

His words were like that of a father scolding his child. He was attempting to send her away as if she had no rights in their man's world. She'd had enough.

"I most certainly will not wait outside," she snapped with a look on her face that instilled fear. "Asher's in no condition to discuss anything with you right now. Anything you need to say to him, you can say it tomorrow." She turned to Asher, who casually sipped his drink and pretended he wasn't listening. The tiny smirk on his face indicated he had been listening and enjoyed her small tirade. "Come on, Asher. Let's get you home."

Asher finished his drink, set the glass down with a cheerful smile at Angel, and tossed her a fifty-dollar tip, indicating he'd been there most of the afternoon.

"Later, Angel."

Asher turned and placed his arm around Jacey's shoulder for added support in an effort to maintain his sober appearance. He nearly succeeded. Nathan was enraged by the verbal lashing and Asher's smug attitude.

"Got you whipped, has she?" Nathan remarked snidely while folding his arms across his chest.

"That's right," Asher replied while grinning. "But don't be jealous, you'll always have Nick."

Nick sneered and made a motion toward Asher, who didn't move but kept his eyes locked on the large man. Despite his obvious drunken condition, Jacey felt Asher tense against her shoulder. She somehow knew he'd be ready to pounce on a moment's notice, and his chances of beating Nick were still better than average.

Nathan casually stopped Nick from engaging Asher in a fight. "Let it go, Nick. The drunken 'has been' is just trying to have a moment."

Jacey appeared annoyed but refrained from commenting. She was already in danger of losing her job as it was. She tugged on Asher, afraid if given enough time he'd accept the challenge or come up with his own.

"Time to go," Jacey announced.

Asher chuckled lowly, clung to Jacey, and waved at the men, his middle finger extended further than the rest in silent gesture. "Good night, boys."

Asher and Jacey left the smoking lounge and entered the hallway. Jacey was just happy to be away from the thick stench of cigar smoke. Nathan and Nick followed them at a distance then headed for the back hallway leading toward the office area. Asher paused before the men's room and smiled at Jacey while pointing to the nearby door.

"I just need to make a side stop in the little boys' room," he cheerfully announced.

She had to grin at his child-like innocence. "That's probably a good idea."

Asher released Jacey and drunkenly stumbled into the nearby men's room.

†

Once Nick passed through the doorway to the reception office, Nathan slammed the door. Nick casually sat on Jacey's desk and glared at his furious boss. Nick obviously had strong feelings on how the incident within the smoking lounge should have panned out and showed his irritation.

"Why didn't you let me have him?" Nick demanded, noting his boss's foul mood matched his.

"Because that wouldn't have looked good for the club, attacking a drunken member, and certainly not in front of Jacey," Nathan remarked then sneered. "She's a Konrad Asher sympathizer. I don't need her going to Davis with something like that." Nathan angrily paced the office while attempting to hold his temper. "Davis is on the fence about bringing Asher on as an investor and board member. I don't want to give him reason to sway in Asher's favor." He glared at Nick. "Keep an eye on those two until they're gone. Make sure they leave. I don't want any more surprises out of that one."

Nick nodded then left the reception area and entered the back hallway. Nathan hurried into his office and slammed the door behind him. He turned on the light alongside the door, brightening the office. Asher stood directly in front of him, startling Nathan. He gasped with alarm and reached for the door behind him. Asher grabbed him by the shirt collar with both hands and slammed him against the wall near the office door. He struck the wall with such force, the frosted glass on the door cracked. Asher stared into Nathan's eyes with an icy glare.

"I promised Jacey I wouldn't get into any trouble in light of recent events," Asher announced in an oddly calm tone without taking his eyes from Nathan, keeping him pinned to the door. "Don't *make* me disappoint her."

Asher released him, straightened Nathan's shirt collar while grinning, and then left the office through the main door. Nathan appeared unnerved then slowly relaxed while releasing his breath. He looked from the door then to the open window with a bewildered expression.

Chapter Twenty-four

Asher's black Audi SUV was parked in front of his dimly lit cabin just a little before eight o'clock that night. Jacey helped Asher into his mostly dark bedroom, not bothering to stop and turn on the lights. Asher appeared less steady on his feet now and clung to her for support. She helped him to the bed, partially pulled down the covers for him, and helped him sit down. He collapsed onto the bed, fell onto his back with his legs dangling over the edge, and moaned while rolling his eyes.

"I'm never drinking again."

Jacey laughed softly, having heard that fairy tale many times before. Although, his whereabouts over the last twenty-four hours did have her curious.

"Have you really been drinking since you left the museum last night?" she asked, figuring he wouldn't remember anything she asked by morning anyway.

"Sadly, yes," he muttered then sighed deeply while strumming his fingers on his abdomen as he stared at the ceiling. "What is this place?"

"It's your bedroom," she replied.

"Oh," he remarked with little emotion. "Remind me to dust the ceiling in the morning."

She knew he wasn't purposely changing the subject, since she doubted his attention span was longer than three seconds, so she pressed with her original line of questioning.

"Your car was at the club since this morning, but I looked everywhere for you," she remarked then eyed him suspiciously. "Where were you hiding?"

"Well, after I closed the smoking lounge bar last night, Jack Daniels and I took a walk behind the club and found a nice little quiet spot in the woods near the ninth hole," he replied. "Sometime late this morning, I had brunch in the Garden Room." He considered his movements that afternoon. "Afterwards, I showered in the gym, although I'm afraid it may have been the ladies' shower room. Then I wondered around for the longest time in a pink towel until I remembered where I'd left my clothes." He hesitated and glanced at his fingernails through the dim lighting. "I vaguely remember getting a manicure." He groaned softly. "I certainly hope that was after I found my clothes."

Jacey groaned and shook her head. She removed his first shoe and dropped it to the floor. As she worked on untying the other shoe, he rubbed her arm with his sock-covered foot while studying her through the dim lighting.

"Are you mad?"

Jacey dropped his second shoe on the floor then sat on the edge of the bed near his knees while facing him.

"Of course not," she announced and offered a tiny smile. "As soon as I get you tucked in, I plan on getting a little plastered myself."

"That's my girl," he announced cheerfully. "Then we can both feel like shit tomorrow."

Asher reached out for her and gently caressed her lower arm while studying her. He smiled charmingly.

"Why do you put up with me?"

She stared back at him. Although she knew the answer, she refrained from responding too quickly. "Because I completely adore you," she replied with a reluctant sigh then smiled, although he probably couldn't see it. "When you're around, you make me feel like I'm the most important person in the room."

Asher slowly sat up, now only inches from her, and met her gaze. Despite the dim lighting, she could still see the blue of his eyes.

"That's because you are the most important person in the room," he announced gently but firm then raised his brows, "--any room."

Asher took her hand in his and gently kissed it, as he had so many times before. Although this time, she noted a little added affection, causing her heart to skip a beat. His eyes never left hers, and she felt compelled to stare helplessly back at him.

"You know I absolutely worship you, my darling," he announced with warmth and affection.

Jacey smiled warmly while staring at him through the dim lighting. She could say the same about him, which probably explained part of why her relationship with Maxwell had failed. Asher had been the most important man in her life for as long as she could remember. He gently brushed the hair from her face then ran the back of his fingers down her cheek before his hand came to rest on her shoulder. Jacey remained motionless and watched him. Although he was normally outwardly affectionate toward her, he tended to ramp up the charm while drinking. She often shamed herself for secretly enjoying those moments, but she liked when he laid on the charm. She often felt it was a small glimpse into what Katie must have felt when they were together. Katie was lucky to have been loved so much by him. Jacey was slightly swept away in the moment as she awaited the warm kiss on her cheek that was bound to follow. She knew he'd then hold her in his arms and the world would be as it should be.

Oddly, he seemed to be lingering for some reason. She gently touched his face then allowed her hand to fall to his chest and remain there. To her surprise, Asher lowered his mouth to hers. Jacey felt her heart suddenly pound in her chest with anticipation. His lips touched hers as he kissed her warmly. It wasn't a quick kiss this time; it was a real kiss. Jacey knew in his drunken condition that he must have thought she was Katie, but she couldn't force herself to stop him. She uncertainly returned the kiss while running her hand up his chest and gently placed her arms around his neck as she moved against him. His kiss turned more passionate, almost startling her, but she couldn't resist returning the passionate kiss. Asher pulled her against him and then lowered her to the bed, placing himself on top of her. Jacey held back her surprised gasp but refused to break off the kiss. Her acceptance was wrong, but the feeling was so incredibly erotic, she didn't want to stop him, although she knew she would have to *eventually*.

His hand firmly caressed her side, ran along her buttocks, and then along her thigh. He pulled her leg up and alongside his hip, gently maneuvering between her legs while now aggressively kissing her. She remained so focused on the kiss; she hadn't even realized he had placed himself between her legs. As he grinded his hips against hers, Jacey gasped at the sensation, now aware of his position. She returned the aggressive kiss while enjoying his aroused state as he grinded rhythmically against her. Between his kiss and the sensation of his hard body pressing against hers, she was dizzy with ecstasy. As his mouth left hers, he warmly kissed her neck and throat while his hands traveled her body, fondling her breast over her shirt. She writhed beneath his body and moaned her pleasure to his firmly caressing hands. She wanted this to happen and made a conscious effort not to stop him. She was torn, because she had to stop him. He thought she was Katie, and it would be wrong to let him continue. Asher stopped kissing her neck, breathed softly in her ear, and then passed out. Jacey attempted to catch her breath and stared at the motionless man on top of her. She attempted to move him off her, but he was dead weight. She groaned softly.

"Terrific."

Chapter Twenty-five

It was a little after nine o'clock that evening. Roxy entered the west wing lounge with Professor, who studied her with concern. She appeared unnerved about something but was reluctant to speak. He offered her a seat on the comfortable sofa toward the back of the room and sat a few feet from her, facing her.

"I appreciate you meeting me, Professor," Roxy announced and fidgeted. "After what happened tonight, I didn't know what else to do."

"You sounded upset on the phone," Professor remarked. "What happened?"

"I'm concerned about what Jacey may have gotten herself into," Roxy announced while staring at him with a look almost resembling fear. "Earlier this evening, I heard Asher was drunk in the smoking lounge. Apparently, he got into a fight with Nathan over something."

"Nothing unusual about that," Professor remarked. "Those two have been going at it since Jacey started working at the country club."

"It's what happened shortly after that has me worried," she announced timidly. "I can't say anything to Jacey, because I know how she feels about Asher, but what happened tonight has me frightened for her."

"Asher's a lot worse in theory then in reality," he announced reassuringly. "You can't listen to the rumors and gossip. His reputation is based on lies."

"Not you too. This has nothing to do with his prior reputation," Roxy insisted. "How am I going to get anyone to listen to me if everyone blindly defends him?"

"I'm sorry, I didn't mean to interrupt," Professor responded delicately. "Please, continue."

She took a deep breath, exhaled, and attempted to compose herself. "When Jacey was about to take him home this evening, I saw Asher go into the men's room. I'd swear he was completely intoxicated, but then he came out of the reception office just five minutes later looking one hundred percent sober. I don't know why, but I decided to follow him. He met up with Jacey in the hallway, and suddenly he was acting drunk again." She fidgeted slightly and shifted on the sofa. "Later, I heard Nathan tell Nick that Asher threatened him in his office." Her eyes pleaded with Professor's. "Asher's up to something."

Professor stared at her a long moment with a strange look as he processed the new information. He appeared to consider her story then shifted on the sofa.

"Jacey and I are pretty close," he remarked casually, although it was evident he was concerned. "I'll talk to her in the morning. Asher has been acting strange lately, but he's been under a lot of stress. I'll see what I can do, okay?"

"Thanks, Professor," Roxy announced and gently touched his lower arm. "I knew I could count on you." She smiled more naturally and stood. Professor stood as well. "You always have the answers to everything."

Professor appeared slightly embarrassed and hid his smile. "Well, maybe not to everything--"

Roxy quickly kissed him on the lips, pulled away, and smiled. "I really appreciate this," she chirped. "Jacey's been a wonderful friend to me even when I refused to believe her about Brian. I just don't want to see her hurt."

"Oh, well, there's one thing you'll never have to worry about," he announced and offered a pleasant smile. "Asher would never hurt Jacey. He adores her."

She shifted uncomfortably and met his gaze. "You know, despite what happened at the museum party, a lot of people still think he murdered his wife."

"People say a lot of things that aren't true," he interjected a little too quickly. "According to Jacey, just before he died, the real killer confessed to killing Asher's wife."

"That makes me feel better," Roxy announced with a gentle sigh and smiled more naturally. "I can't imagine Jacey lying about something like that, not even to protect Asher's reputation."

She kissed him once more and prolonged it. As she pulled back, Professor stared at her with surprise. Roxy gave him a quick, embarrassed smile, waved, and then headed for the main door. Professor watched her leave then touched his lips. He could barely contain his grin then sighed.

"She's certainly friendly these days," Professor muttered. He hesitated and sank into thought. "Jacey lie to protect Asher--?" Professor scratched his head while remaining deep in thought. "I don't think she would, but then again--"

†

Roxy hurried from the west wing to her car that was parked between Professor's black, Lexus sedan and Brian's red Corvette. The parking area was brightly lit, although there were shadows only a few yards away. She heard a twig snap from within the darkness near the side of the building. Roxy looked around with concern. There didn't appear to be anyone around.

"Professor?"

There was no response. She fumbled with her keys and unlocked her car door. As she looked past her car, she saw a shadow move near the edge of the main building. She stared a moment longer, appeared curious, and then saw a tree branch moving slightly in the breeze, casting shadows on the building. She sighed with relief and opened her car door.

†

After Roxy had left, Professor walked across the dimly lit lobby exhibit. He neared the yellow-taped police line, eyed it, and then took a wide birth around it. He heard a faint crash. Professor looked toward the door to the scientist's labs near the back of the main museum. He slowly walked toward the door marked 'lab' and reached for the doorknob then hesitated. He saw it was partially open when it was usually kept shut. A floorboard creaked from nearby, startling him. Professor quickly turned and nearly collided with Timon. Both cried out and jumped with alarm. Timon clutched his chest and gasped.

"Damn it, you nearly killed me!" Timon cried out.

"What are you doing sneaking around so late at night?" Professor demanded and felt his own chest in response.

"You're the one sneaking around--and with girls," Timon snapped. "What was Roxy doing here at this hour?"

"Nothing, she just wanted me to talk to Jacey about Asher's behavior."

Rather than seeming curious, Timon appeared offended. "Why didn't she ask me? I'm closer to Jacey then you are."

"You are not," Professor scoffed.

"Am too."

"She probably figured I can handle the conversation more delicately than you."

"Yeah, and it'll take hours for her to even figure out what it is you've said," Timon remarked.

"I see you're feeling your old self," Professor muttered then indicated the partially open door. "Is someone downstairs in the lab?"

"Shouldn't be," Timon announced. "With Doc and Maxwell gone, it's just us."

They eyed one another then appeared uneasy and looked back at the police line surrounding the t-rex. They exchanged looks and simultaneously tensed.

"Maybe we should lock ourselves in the west wing," Timon suggested.

"I heard a crash from the lab," Professor informed him. "Think we should check it out?"

"No," he announced while vigorously shaking his head, "I don't." Timon attempted to turn and leave.

Professor grabbed his arm and stopped him, although he wasn't easy to hold back.

"All my research is down there," Professor announced firmly. "You're coming with me."

Professor pulled open the door and politely extended his hand, indicating for Timon to go first. Timon raised his brows daringly and extended his hand in response. Professor frowned and passed through the doorway before him. Both headed down the stairs to the basement labs. They stopped at the bottom of the broad stairs and looked around the dimly lit area. Professor turned on the lights, brightening the large lab. The offices along the outer edge remained dark. The glass on one of the doors was shattered and the door was partially open. Both stared at the dark office. They glanced around the lab for signs of an intruder, but they appeared to be alone. Professor snatched a blowtorch from the nearby lab table. Timon grabbed a plastic dinosaur femur bone and clutched it in a deadly fashion above his head. Professor gave him a bewildered stare then looked back at the broken door and flicked the blowtorch on. Professor and Timon slowly approached the dark office with their weapons. Professor nervously reached inside the open door and flipped the light switch. The office brightened. Brian's office had been moderately trashed, but it was mostly papers that lie scattered around the room. Professor and Timon stared at the ransacked office with shared looks of concern.

"I think it's time to call Sheriff Monroe," Timon softly remarked.

"I think you're right."

Chapter Twenty-six

Later the following morning, Jacey walked through the lobby exhibit from the kitchen area with Professor while he sipped his morning coffee. Judging by the dark circles under Professor's eyes, it looked as if he'd lost a lot of sleep after last night's break-in. Both paused near the t-rex and stared at the police line surrounding it. The blood had been cleaned, but there was a faint bloodstain that was still visible, reminding them of Brian's brutal killing. They exhaled simultaneously without comment then continued toward the west wing and entered the lounge.

"I can't believe someone broke into Brian's office," Jacey remarked while gently rubbing her chilled shoulders as she eyed the tall man. "Was anything missing?"

"It's hard to say. He seemed to be looking for something in Brian's files. Who, apart from another scientist, would have any interest in Brian's files?" he remarked while momentarily drifting out. He snapped back into reality. "Nothing was missing that Timon or I could tell." He sighed and shook his head, withholding his groan.

"Timon's really freaked out over this. I think he still blames himself for Brian."

"We've all been through a lot," she remarked gently. "I know how he feels."

"I'm still trying to forget our last deadly fundraiser, and I wasn't even there for the after party," Professor muttered then glanced at her as they crossed the lounge to the sofa. He appeared slightly tense but spoke regardless. "I heard Asher got drunk at the club last night and started a fight with Nathan."

Jacey suddenly groaned and glared at him. "That's not true," she protested. "Nathan tried to pick a fight with Asher. He knew he was drunk and thought he'd be an easy target. Asher took the high road--" She hesitated and considered the comment. "--for once."

"Somehow I doubt Asher's an easy target even while unconscious," Professor teased.

Both collapsed on the sofa. Professor propped his large feet on the coffee table, allowed his head to fall back, and groaned softly. He then eyed her from his reclined position.

"Your town is cursed," he remarked. "You know that, right?"

She stared at him a moment in silence. "Well, it's finally happened. You're officially a member of Stony Ridge," she scoffed then raised her brows. "And I mean that in the rudest possible way."

"Our transfer here was the beginning of a very rocky start to my new career," he replied casually.

Both were unusually quiet. Jacey still had a lot on her mind as she stared blankly at the coffee table and Professor's excessively big feet. Professor seemed to realize she hadn't commented and then studied her.

"So, uh, has Asher still been acting, uh, odd?"

Jacey sharply looked at Professor with surprise by the comment. She wondered if he somehow read her mind. Professor noted her look and appeared concerned.

"Is something wrong?" he asked while placing his feet on the floor as he sat forward.

Jacey leaned back on the sofa, covered her eyes, and groaned softly. She didn't want to confess to anyone what had happened between them last night, but she suddenly felt the need to blurt it out.

"Oh, Professor," she gasped softly. "I don't know what to do."

Professor turned on the sofa to face her and placed his hand on her shoulder. "What happened? You'll feel better if you confide in me."

She sighed and sat forward then stared at him. "Well, you already heard Asher was a little drunk at the club last night, and that I drove him home. He was pretty unsteady, so I helped put him to bed." She hesitated then fidgeted. "He must've thought I was Katie, and, uh, he kissed me."

Jacey uncertainly met his gaze. Professor stared at her a moment with shock and moderate alarm.

"He, uh, kissed you?" Professor pointed to his mouth. "As in--?"

Jacey groaned. "Oh, yeah--"

Professor removed his hand from her shoulder and appeared uncomfortable. "Oh, boy. Uh, you probably shouldn't say anything to him if he doesn't remember. You'll just make him feel bad." Professor hesitated then muttered, "Then he'll be in a *real* bad mood. No one wants him in a bad mood."

She shifted slightly and held back her grimace. "That's not the worst part," Jacey announced softly then squirmed in her seat. "I sort of kissed him back."

"You mean--?" His eyes widened and he almost couldn't speak. "Oh, wow."

Jacey groaned and allowed her head to fall into her hands. "I don't know what I was thinking." She then lifted her head and started to ramble. "I mean, I obviously wasn't thinking. I don't know; maybe I was thinking. I still can't believe I did that!"

After taking a moment for her words to sink in, Professor inhaled deeply and turned reassuring. "There's nothing to be ashamed about, Jacey. It's not the end of the world," Professor informed her. "With how drunk he was, he probably won't even remember."

"No, Professor, that's not it," she announced softly. "I'm ashamed because I *enjoyed* it."

Professor stared at her with complete surprise and was at a loss for words. Jacey ran her fingers through her hair and drifted out a moment.

"When I was younger, I had a terrible crush on Asher," she explained gently. "I mean, I've always been attracted to his strength, and I've always felt completely safe whenever he'd put his arms around me. But I never expected--" She hesitated then inhaled deeply. "When he kissed me, it was like nothing I'd ever felt before.

It was almost intoxicating. I just wanted to crawl inside him and never come out. It just felt so *natural*."

Professor stared at her a long moment in silence. Jacey looked at him with some embarrassment. She wished he'd say something. Anything would do. She smiled gently and fought her tears.

"Heaven help me; I think I'm in love with him." She sniffed and wiped a tear from the corner of her eye. "And if I'm honest with myself, I think I have been for a very long time."

Professor snapped out of his dazed state and shook his head vigorously while staring with concern. "Jacey, he thinks of you as his daughter," he finally gasped. "You can't tell him any of this. It'll destroy him."

"I know, that's why I never allowed myself to feel this way, but I don't know how to go back," she remarked. "Every time I look at him, I'm going to think about last night and what almost happened."

"There was an *almost happened?*" Professor asked while raising his brows. He suddenly became animated and threw his hands around. "No, no, no! If he finds out you're thinking thoughts like that about him, he'll go psycho. He's already on his way toward some sort of breakdown." Professor drew a deep breath and collected his emotions. "You need to hope he doesn't remember any of it. Let him think it was all a dream about Kate. The world will be a much happier place, trust me."

"I know you're right," she muttered softly.

Jacey uncertainly stood and subconsciously ran her fingers through her hair several times. Professor jumped to his feet to join her.

"I have to take care of the horses then think about what I'm going to do about Asher," she remarked timidly and remained deep in thought. "If I act even slightly off, he'll know something is wrong. He's extremely perceptive. It's what I love and hate about him." She shook her head and groaned softly. "I almost wish it wasn't Saturday. If I had to work, it'd be a good excuse to avoid him altogether."

Professor gently massaged Jacey's shoulder as he walked with her to the front entrance. "It's going to be okay, Jacey," he announced with warmth and sincerity. "I promise. Everything will work out just fine."

Once they reached the door, Jacey turned to face him. "Thanks, Professor," she announced gently. "I needed to talk to someone. I barely slept last night. I couldn't get what happened off my mind."

"Absolutely, I understand," he replied sympathetically. "You know I'm always here for you."

They exchanged a quick hug. She smiled gently and then left the lounge. Professor shut the door behind her then leaned his back against it. He stared blankly a moment at nothing and didn't move for the longest time.

"Jacey's in love with Asher," he announced with a sigh then straightened and shook his head. "There goes my chances with her."

The phone on the nearby hall table rang, breaking the silence, and nearly startled him. Professor approached the table and picked up the phone.

"Hello?" He hesitated as he listened then appeared concerned by the call. "Roxy, what's wrong? You sound upset." He listened to Roxy chatter on the other end then nodded. "Yeah, I can meet you at the club." He listened to her then looked at his watch. "Uh, yeah. Sure, I can be there in fifteen minutes."

Professor hung up the phone and appeared confused by the call. He jotted a note for Timon on a tablet by the phone then turned and headed for the door.

†

At the same time, Roxy hung up the phone on her desk within the reception office. She looked nervous and moderately stressed after having spoken with Professor. Nathan entered the room from his office, startling her. He gripped a manila envelope in his hand then relaxed and gave her a bewildered look. She faked a smile but seemed uncomfortable that he may have overheard her conversation with Professor. It made sense that none of the guys would be in their offices on the weekend, so it was odd that he had been in his at that particular moment.

"What are you doing working on a Saturday?" Nathan suddenly asked.

"My father came in for a few hours, so I thought I'd come in with him and catch up on some filing," she remarked while attempting to hide her nervousness.

Nathan gave her an odd look then smiled pleasantly and leaned on her desk.

"What are you doing for lunch?"

"Uh, probably having lunch with my father," she responded with tension in her voice.

"I thought maybe you and I could discuss something I'd found with Brian's things," Nathan announced with a sly grin on his face.

She glared at him, becoming impatient and irritable. "I'm sorry Brian is dead. He didn't deserve that, but I'm not interested in anything you have of his."

"This might interest you," he announced and tossed the manila envelope onto her desk.

She groaned softly, picked up the envelope, and pulled out the photos.

Nathan continued the conversation in a jovial tone. "It would seem Brian's affair with Angel wasn't the only scandal waiting to rock your world," he teased.

Roxy saw enough of the top photo to see Jeannette's naked body in bed with someone. Judging by the scenery, it was obviously taken in Jeannette's bedroom. Roxy held her breath, obviously upset by what she saw then returned them to the envelope without looking at the rest of the X-rated photo. She glared at Nathan while extending the envelope to him.

"These are of no interest to me," she announced proudly. "If it's blackmail you're attempting, you should know that I don't care what you do with those pictures." A realization must have hit her. She suddenly stood and glared into his eyes with surprise. "It was you, wasn't it? You're the one I saw sneaking around the museum last night." She appeared surprised then shook her head. "That's where you got those photos, isn't it? You stole them from Brian's office!"

Nathan didn't react to the accusation, but his body tensed slightly.

She suddenly smiled and laughed. "Oh, my father's going to love hearing that." She straightened and smiled proudly. "A word of advice, Nathan. *Never* attempt to blackmail your business partner's daughter. Imagine my father's reaction when I tell him everything I know. So really, who has whom over the barrel here?" She raised her brows then sneered at him. "Now, if you'll excuse me, I have a lot of work to do."

Roxy grabbed a stack of folders from the desk. Nathan dropped the envelope on top of her folders. She glared at him as he smiled smugly.

"In case you reconsider," he announced with a little more confidence. "And you might be surprised to find it's you who's over that barrel."

Roxy gave him a look of disgust and stormed from the room with her stack of folders and the envelope. Nathan watched her leave and snickered softly.

Chapter Twenty-seven

Roxy sat on the old bench with a stack of papers alongside her awaiting to be filed. Instead of filing, she held the envelope containing the black and white photos. She slammed the photos face down on the envelope and appeared enraged by them. Their significance should have been irrelevant, but the look on Roxy's face conveyed something more personal. She heard someone moving around within the file room. Roxy became concerned, quickly stood, and hid the envelope within the filing folder. She slowly approached the end of the aisle and looked around the shelves. There was no one there.

"Hello? Professor?" she called out then paused to listen a moment. "Is that you?"

There was no response. Roxy appeared tense and quickly returned to her stack of papers and folders. She returned the photos to the large envelope and turned it over. The printed writing on the front simply read, 'to my love'. Roxy heard more movement within the file room, which couldn't have been coincidental. She spun around and looked back at the aisle opening. Roxy appeared concerned and again approached the end of the aisle.

†

Forty minutes after he'd received the urgent phone call from Roxy, Professor entered the reception office and saw Carl sitting behind Jacey's desk, routing through her drawers. When he saw Professor in the doorway, he jumped with surprise then attempted to cover with a false smile.

"What brings you here, Professor?" Carl asked. "It's Saturday. Jacey's off for the weekend."

Professor scanned the office with a calm look then eyed Carl. "Actually, I was looking for Roxy. Have you seen her?"

"Roxy? No, she's off for the weekend as well," he announced and leaned back in Jacey's chair. "I'm just catching up on some leftover business from Friday myself. Davis is here somewhere. Maybe he knows where Roxy is."

"Actually, she called me from here and asked me to meet her for lunch."

"Oh, then she's probably in the Garden Room."

"No," he replied. "I checked there first."

"Have you checked the file room?" Carl questioned while studying the tall man. "That's where Jacey always goes when she doesn't want to be found."

"The file room? Where's that?"

"Just down the hall in the basement," Carl replied. "You can't miss the door."

Professor nodded while giving Carl a suspicious look then left the reception area. Carl leaned back in the chair and appeared relieved. Davis entered the office, looked at Carl, and then pointed toward the door.

"Was that Professor?" Davis asked. "What's he doing here so early on a Saturday?"

"He said he was meeting Roxy for lunch," Carl offered then quickly stood. His look conveyed his concerns as he stared at Davis. "I found something in Nathan's office. You're not going to like it." Carl handed Davis a manila envelope with the words, "to my love" printed on the front.

Davis opened it and looked at the photos. His expression immediately dropped to what he saw then shoved the photos back into the envelope.

"What's the meaning of this?" Davis demanded with rage in his eyes as he waved the envelope.

"I'm not sure," Carl replied almost timidly, obviously not wanting to upset his partner, "but I'm guessing Nathan intends to use them against your daughter."

"What?" he nearly shouted. "You think he plans to blackmail my daughter with this?" He shook his head then slammed the envelope into Carl's chest. "When I see that bastard, we're going to have words." Davis appeared unnerved and ran his fingers through his hair. "I need to find my daughter and tell her about this before she hears it from Nathan." He then glared at Carl and pointed a threatening finger at him. "If you see Nathan, you tell him I want to talk to him."

Carl nodded in response. Davis turned and hurried from the office. Carl eyed the envelope then dropped it on the desk while groaning softly.

"Oh, Nathan," he muttered. "I wouldn't want to be in your shoes." A strange, twisted smile crossed Carl's face. He held back his chuckle.

†

Professor appeared at the bottom of the rickety old steps in the file room then paused and looked around. There wasn't any sound, although how much sound did filing actually make? The file room was eerie, as were most basements, and it made Professor slightly uneasy.

"Hello?"

There was no response. The room wasn't that big. If Roxy were downstairs, she would have heard him. Despite a lack of response, he walked along the main aisle and peered into each side aisle as he passed. He paused at the back of the file room and saw a folder containing scattered papers and an envelope with photos beneath it. It appeared as if someone had left in a hurry. Professor again looked around, this time with added concern. He looked back at the scattered papers and the envelope with the photos. The photos caught his attention. He entered the aisle, crouched down, and sifted through the black and white photos in the plain, unmarked manila envelope. As he studied the pictures of Asher with Brian, obviously taken from a spy cam, someone stepped into the aisle behind him. He heard someone approaching and was about to straighten when he was struck on the head with a baton style flashlight. Professor barely had time to gasp before collapsing the rest of the way to the floor.

Chapter Twenty-eight

It was early afternoon by the time Jacey returned to Asher's cabin with his borrowed Audi SUV. After stopping to visit Professor, she had gone to her house to feed the horses. It seemed unlikely that Asher would be up before noon anyway. Jacey entered the front sitting room with Asher's keys dangling from her finger. The large, front sitting room was the more formal less used room in the house with expensive, barely touched furniture. She personally had never sat on the furniture. When she visited Asher, they spent most of their time in the sunroom, which was Asher's preferred room. Jacey shut the door behind her, laid the keys on the nearby table, and headed across the room.

"Asher, I'm back," she called out.

There was no response, which wasn't surprising. She could see him sleeping most of the day after his 24-hour bender. Jacey entered the back hallway and approached his bedroom. The bedroom door was open and the room was relatively dark with the curtains drawn to keep out the dreary morning. As Jacey entered, she looked at the already made bed and was surprised that he was up, considering the night he had. She heard the shower running and approached the bathroom.

"Asher, I'm back," she called through the closed bathroom door.

There was still no response, but she didn't think much of it. Jacey headed across the room, noticed something on the dresser that seemed out of place, and approached. The last remaining framed photo of Katie within the house now lie face down on top of the dresser. Jacey picked up the picture, studied it a moment, and then replaced it to its usual position on the dresser. Her eyes strayed to the carved, wooden antique jewelry box. A man's platinum wedding band lie on top. Jacey uncertainly picked up the wedding band and stared at it with bewilderment. She was deep in thought and didn't even notice the shower has stopped. Jacey looked back at the picture of Katie and wondered what was going through Asher's head. Why had the picture been turned down? Why had he removed the rest of her pictures? What was up with his wedding ring? The questions were nagging at her.

"What do you have there?" came Asher's voice.

She saw a brief image of Asher in the bathroom doorway through the dresser mirror. Jacey replaced the ring to the top of the box, turned to face him, and attempted a tiny smile. She took in an eyeful of him in the bathroom doorway wearing just an old pair of shorts. She didn't often seen him without his shirt. Although not excessively muscular, he maintained a solid build with a light coating of chest hair. The scars along his upper body were plentiful enough to play tic-tac-toe. He'd seen plenty of action during his tour with the CIA. The newest scar on his shoulder was a reminder of the museum party gone bad, reminding her how he saved her life while taking a bullet meant for her.

"Just looking at Katie's picture."

Asher smiled gently with a slight nod but didn't comment. He approached his closet and casually opened it.

"I'd wondered what became of my car," he announced. "I called the club, but no one answered." Asher removed a shirt and a pair of pants then glanced at her. "I feared I'd be stranded here all day."

"More like you were about to call a cab and hunt me down," Jacey replied.

He chuckled softly. "You're probably right."

Asher tossed his clothes on the bed then approached her and the dresser. Jacey appeared uneasy and moved out of his way. He removed a pair of underwear and socks then casually turned Katie's picture face down once again. He turned toward Jacey with a casual smile that seemed to mock her.

"We could continue this conversation while I dress, but it might be a bit awkward for you."

Jacey appeared embarrassed and forced a smile while blushing. A few thoughts bounced around inside her mind, which she quickly dismissed. She pointed to the bedroom door.

"I'll be making coffee," Jacey announced then slipped from the bedroom.

Chapter Twenty-nine

The rain poured against the glass sunroom windows. They were having a severe thunderstorm, but it would pass soon and give away to late afternoon sunshine. Jacey sat on the floor while resting her back against the wicker sofa. She held a mug of coffee while flipping through an old photo album usually kept beneath the coffee table for easy access. Asher didn't have many photo albums, just those from the three-year period he'd been with Katie. Before Stony Ridge, it seemed as if he didn't exist. His secret stint with the CIA may have had something to do with that. Jacey was the only one in town who knew about Asher's secret past. Asher entered the room with a mug of coffee in his hand. He paused, looked at her where she sat, and then joined her on the floor. After last night, she couldn't deny she enjoyed his closeness a little more than usual. He propped his elbow on the sofa near her and rested his temple on his knuckles while watching her.

"You have a strange fascination for photos today," he casually remarked.

She glanced at him and grinned in response. "Photos are the door to a person's past," Jacey announced then sighed while looking at a photo of Asher with Katie. "You must've made Katie very happy."

Asher glanced at the album in her hands. He gently removed the album from her, shut it, and placed it on the sofa behind him.

Jacey gave him a strange look. It was odd behavior. Of course, he'd been behaving oddly for the last three months. Katie had always been his favorite subject, but lately, he seemed reluctant even to mention her name. His behavior was starting to get the better of her, and she decided it was time to call him on it.

"Don't care for the topic?" she asked while raising her brows in question.

"Just closing the door."

Jacey studied him a moment with some uncertainty. She turned onto her hip, leaned her elbow on the sofa, and faced him. She stared into his blue eyes and attempted to get a read on the hard to read man.

"What's bothering you, Asher?"

"Nothing's bothering me," he announced while grinning and stared back at her. "What's bothering you?"

Jacey casually took his left hand and held it up, revealing the indent where his wedding band had once been for many years. Asher ran his thumb over the indent then gently pulled his hand away. He smiled casually.

"Just another fond memory," he informed her. "Why does it bother you?"

"She was the most important part of your life," Jacey replied and tilted her head while giving him a curious look. "Have you lost that?"

Asher smiled at her then stood and approached the stereo in the corner. He turned on a slow song then returned to Jacey and extended his hand to her. Jacey accepted his hand, stood, and allowed him to pull her into his arms for a slow dance. Jacey enjoyed his suave style of slow dancing. The first time she had ever danced with Asher was at the museum gala. Of course, it was also the first time someone had tried to kill her too. He gracefully dipped her, causing her to smile and laugh softly. As he pulled her back up and into his arms, they danced closer.

"No one dips quite like you," she teased.

"Please submit all compliments in writing and leave them at the front desk."

Asher smiled, gracefully dipped her deep, and held her there a moment. He brought her back up, spun them slightly, and continued to dance close. Jacey smiled with a soft laugh and touched his face. He took her hand, gently kissed it, and once more held it to his chest. She placed her head on his shoulder and enjoyed the way his body gently brushed past hers as they slow danced. Her body ached with desire, wanting to feel him once more pressed against her.

Images of their brief encounter last night filled her thoughts, and she didn't know how to make them stop.

"It's nice having you all to myself again," he teased, breaking her out of her fantasy.

Jacey lifted her head slightly and brushed her cheek against his. "You never were big on sharing."

"Maxwell was far too possessive," he remarked without care. "You already have me. There's no room for two possessive men in your life." He considered then sighed deeply. "Can't trust the quiet, shy type, I suppose."

"Exactly what type would suit you?" she asked while meeting his gaze with a teasing grin.

He considered the comment and withheld his chuckle. "Maybe I'll just get you a puppy instead."

Jacey rolled her eyes and returned her head to his shoulder. She brushed her lips gently past his cheek then cursed herself for her actions.

"I don't want a puppy, and I certainly don't want your help finding a man," she remarked simply. "I have my hands full with you."

Both danced a moment longer in silence. Asher gently caressed her back while they slow danced and avoided looking at her. Something was troubling him. She could almost feel his body tense as he inhaled deeply.

"Should I bring up my behavior last night or are we pretending nothing happened?" he finally asked.

Jacey pulled away to meet his gaze with a look of concern and surprise as they stopped dancing. She was suddenly uneasy and moderately embarrassed that he had remembered, which meant he also remembered she didn't exactly put up a fight either. She possibly had more reason to be embarrassed than he did. Asher remained his usual, casual self as he stared into her eyes awaiting a response.

"I didn't think you'd remember, so I didn't see the point in mentioning it."

"You'd cover for me no matter what wrong I did, this I'm convinced," he responded almost proudly. He tilted his head and appeared curious. "Not feeling betrayed?"

"You were drunk and mistook me for Katie," she replied gently. "I understand."

Asher chuckled lowly and appeared slightly humored. "Would you really like to believe that?" he asked while raising his brow. "You seem to think Katie is the only woman I think about."

He hesitated then sighed softly. "I'd like to keep that fantasy alive for you, darling, but Katie's just a fond memory of a wonderful three years. She was a very long time ago."

She couldn't help but stare into his eyes after the seemingly harsh comment, although she wasn't certain how to respond. Thankfully, he didn't give her the option.

"I've known you three times longer than I had Katie," he announced simply. "To be honest; if she came through that door right now and I had to choose between you and her, I'd choose you, darling."

She was rendered almost speechless by the comment, although it did make her feel special. "That's quite a compliment from you."

Asher smiled warmly, pulled her into his arms, and held her against him in a warm embrace. She clung to him and enjoyed the warmth of his arms around her and his body firmly pressed against hers.

"Darling, I'd walk through the gates of hell for you," he announced then hesitated. "I'd do anything for you. I'd even go away forever, if you asked me too."

Jacey pulled away just far enough to stare into his eyes. She smiled and affectionately caressed his chest. She could feel her heart pounding as the words rolled around in her head. She was almost in disbelief when she spoke them aloud.

"Would you make love to me if I asked you to?" she softly questioned.

Asher appeared slightly surprised by the question and stared at her a moment while unusually silent. As she stared into his blue eyes, she could feel his entire body tense against hers, causing her to momentarily panic. She feared his reaction to her words and regretted having said them. His arms tightened around her waist as he firmly caressed her back.

"Without hesitation," he whispered softly then drew a sharp breath. "But the price would be steep. I'd require a 'til death do us part' clause."

There was an awkward silence as they stared at each other, uncertain if either had been serious. Neither looked away. Jacey ran her hand firmly along his chest and smiled timidly.

"Happily."

For a moment, he could only stare at her then appeared curious. "Did I just ask you to marry me?" he suddenly questioned. "But more importantly, did you just say 'yes'?"

"Without thinking twice," she replied softly.

He stared at her only a brief moment before pulling her against him. Asher kissed her passionately and with moderate aggression that she'd never felt before. Although his aggressive kiss took her by surprise, her entire body ached for him. She tightened her arms around his neck and returned the kiss with urgency. As his hands firmly traveled her body, their kiss turned more aggressive. Her heart was pounding, and she felt a little lightheaded. For a moment, she feared Asher was too much man for her. Her sexual experience was severely limited, while she imagined Asher being an American version of James Bond. As if sensing her apprehensions, Asher broke off the kiss. He kept his mouth close to hers while breathing heavily.

"Are you sure?" he asked softly. "I don't want you to feel pressured."

His words reminded her that she had nothing to fear with him. He wasn't a horny teenager looking to score. This was Asher, her best friend. She relaxed in his arms then gently brushed her lips past his.

"You're the one thing I've always been sure about," she replied softly then looked up to meet his gaze.

Asher groaned and kissed her with great passion and affection. He swept her off her feet and into his arms without breaking off the kiss. Asher effortlessly carried her to his bedroom and lowered her to the bed. He continued kissing her with a wild passion she had never felt before. Her head was spinning and everything after that was a complete blur. Jacey felt almost drunk with desire. She didn't remember taking off her clothes or how he managed to slip out of his seemingly unnoticed; she just remembered feeling his naked body against hers. She never felt such pleasure before. The sensation of his hands caressing her body had her writhing with ecstasy. She heard him speaking to her in his soothing, monotone voice. He repeatedly asked 'are you okay' and said 'stop me if it hurts'.

Jacey heard the questions, but she was so enthralled with his hands caressing her in places she'd never allowed any man before, she could barely murmur a response. His earlier aggression aside, he didn't rush the moment and took his time to ensure her comfort. Her body accepted him without hesitation, welcoming every action and movement. Despite a moment of discomfort, his body against hers and his mouth kissing sensitive spots along her body kept her from acknowledging it. The discomfort had quickly passed, and she could feel her heart pounding in rhythm with his. Her head continued to spin with ecstasy even after their lovemaking had finally died down.

Jacey and Asher clung to each other beneath the sheets as they kissed warmly but passionately, both moderately exhausted. They breathed heavily while attempting to recover from their lengthy round of passion. She'd finally lost her virginity, although she never would have imagined it would be with Asher. It was possibly the single greatest experience in her young life, yet she could barely remember everything that had happened. It was followed by warm kisses, gentle caresses, and another round of him questioning how she felt. She felt great! She wasn't sure what other women experienced during their first time, but Asher was perfect. He was gentle and passionate until the very end when he displayed a brief moment of wild aggression. If she was truthful, she enjoyed the wildly aggressive part most. She wondered if it would be expecting too much to have a repeat performance later, after his heart rate slowed enough to convince her he wasn't going to have a heart attack.

They lay there for several minutes in each other's arms just listening to the sound of their pounding hearts. Jacey's hair was mussed, wildly flowing across Asher's chest, as she rested her head on his shoulder while he held her. Asher finally seemed to come back to life, brushed the hair away from her face, and met her gaze with a sly grin.

"What have I done to you?" he teased. "You look like you've been through hell."

She was glad the old Asher had returned, allowing him to tease with her rather than continually asking if she felt okay. Jacey smiled in response to his remark.

"At least your version of it."

Asher chuckled lowly in his throat and appeared eager to accept the challenge. "As soon as I get my strength back, you're getting it."

She maintained her humor and again nuzzled his chest. "You'll need a lot more than strength in order to give it to me again."

Asher glared at her then cast her onto her back and moved on top of her. She let out a surprised scream then mocked him with a soft laugh.

"Told you so," she teased.

Asher pulled her lower body against his. Jacey let out a surprised gasp. Asher chuckled lowly and kissed her shoulder while moving against her.

"Never doubt me."

Chapter Thirty

It was already early evening, and the happy couple had spent the better part of their day in bed. Jacey's attempt to wash turned into a couple's shower, so her actual cleanliness was in doubt. Since both of them were making up for lost time, she'd worry about a real shower later. Once they had dressed, Jacey realized she was starving. She hadn't eaten since early yesterday afternoon. Naturally, there was little to be found in Asher's cupboards. Once Asher had finished dressing, she saw him enter his study. Jacey entered the disarrayed room only a few seconds behind him, looked at his moderately cluttered desk, and shook her head. The answering machine light blinked demandingly, although Asher seemed contented to ignore it. Jacey was actually surprised at the large amount of unopened mail sitting on the corner of his desk. Nothing about him seemed disorganized, so she found it odd that his study looked as it did. Asher routed through the large stack of mail, looking for something in particular.

"What is all of this?" she asked and picked up a few of the letters that fell to the floor.

He eyed the letters in her hand and grinned. "Fan mail," he teased.

She glared at him. "You mean death threats."

"No, not necessarily true," he protested then casually added, "some are blackmail."

Jacey wanted to comment but didn't bother. "Considering the state of the rest of your house, I'm surprised you've allowed this much junk to accumulate in here."

"Actually, the post office delivered my mail yesterday," he informed her. "I had them hold it while I was away. I didn't have time to sort through it yet." He hesitated then grinned. "You know, being on a bender and all." Asher straightened and scanned his messy desk. "I know there's a travel booklet around here somewhere." He looked back at her and grinned. "Perhaps we'll look through it later and pick someplace warm and tropical to honeymoon."

"With horseback riding on the beach?"

He took her hand and kissed it warmly. "Anything you want, darling."

Ironically, for as much as things were about to change for them, they seemed oddly similar to the way they had been. A strange thought then occurred to her as she stared blankly at the mound of mail. She finally looked back at him with the question she had to ask.

"Asher," she asked gently. "When did you intend to tell me how you really felt?"

He didn't bother looking at her and took no time to consider the question before responding. "Never," he replied and then met her gaze. "I've been hiding those feelings for the last three years. It seemed foolish to risk losing what we had over my selfish desires. I felt it was for the best."

She stared at him with surprise. "That would've been unfair and wrong," she remarked, feeling a little cheated that he never intended to share his feelings. "Ten years from now, we could still be playing these games."

He studied her a moment as if understanding her logic but not necessarily agreeing with it. "Not exactly a topic we can debate in a few minutes," he informed her while maintaining his playful grin. "We'll have to continue this conversation over a romantic dinner with champagne." He considered the comment. "I'll definitely need to find some champagne." Asher looked at her and grinned. "Then, maybe later, a bubble bath." He then sank into his own thoughts. "I really should have that tub replaced in the master bath. A garden tub for two might be a wise investment."

Jacey smiled, held back her laugh, and kissed him warmly on the lips. "You are charming."

"I'll have to pull some strings if we're going to get reservations for dinner at the country club on a Saturday night," he remarked with a soft sigh. He then looked back at her with great affection and pulled her into his arms. "Then we'll come back here and start working on forever."

She gently ran her hands along his chest and met his gaze. "Sounds like a long night."

"Hmm," he agreed. "I intend to keep you in bed all weekend."

He kissed her quickly but passionately then slowly pulled away and turned to his answering machine. He pressed the 'play' button on the machine.

"First--to see what my adoring fans want."

The first message played. "Damn it, Asher," Professor proclaimed from the machine. "Turn your ringer on. I'm looking for Jacey. I'll try her house again."

Asher smiled teasingly and glanced at Jacey. "Your adoring fan."

"Asher, it's Timon," came the second message. "Is Jacey there? I've been trying to locate Professor." They could hear the concern in his tone. "It's not like him to be gone so long without checking in. He left a note this morning about having lunch with Roxy at the club. When I called there, they said his car was there, but no one's seen him. Call me."

As the message ended, Jacey and Asher eyed each other with matching expression.

"I don't like the sound of that," Jacey announced with concern.

"If we're lucky, Professor and Roxy had the same sort of afternoon as we had," he announced then inhaled deeply. "Although I'd better go to the club and check it out."

"I'm going with you," she quickly chirped.

"No, I think you'd better wait here," he announced firmly then frowned. "This has that all too familiar 'institute gala revisited' feel to it."

"All the more reason for me--"

"--to wait here," he replied firmly while raising his brows. "Bolt the door behind me. I'll call you when I find Professor." He then indicated the phone. "Why don't you call Timon? Tell him I'm heading to the club."

Without waiting for a response, he kissed her quickly but passionately, smiled, and then left the room. Jacey frowned and looked back at the cluttered desk. She didn't like being excluded, especially if Asher was about to do something that could get him into trouble. She didn't know why she felt the need to protect him. He didn't need her protection. He was able to get in and out of trouble just fine on his own. Still--?

Jacey saw a travel brochure near the bottom of the mail pile and eagerly pulled it out. At least it'd give her something to do. The pile scattered to the floor. She groaned at her own clumsiness and picked up the fallen mail. To her surprise, she saw a padded envelope on the floor with handwriting that looked suspiciously like Jeannette's, but that wasn't possible. She picked up the envelope with just the city, state, and zip as the return address. Jacey straightened and studied the envelope in her hand. Why did that envelope look so much like those Davis would receive with 'confidential' written across them? She felt a small object between the bubble padding. It only took a moment for her to decide whether or not she should open Asher's private mail. She carefully opened the envelope and stared at the flash drive. She looked around the office and frowned.

Asher certainly didn't own a computer. It was not as if he was eager to join in on social networking. Unfortunately, she was the second to last person in the world who didn't own a computer, which was why she did most of her articles on the computer at the library. There were several computers at the museum, and she was sure Timon or Professor would let her view the contents of the flash drive there. Jacey studied the flash drive a moment, considered its possible contents, and then stuck it down the front of her shirt for safekeeping. The phone on the desk rang, startling her. Jacey relaxed and picked up the cordless phone.

"Hello?"

"Jacey, I'm glad I caught you," Timon announced. "Have you seen Professor?"

"Uh, no," she replied. "Asher got your message. He was going to the country club to look for him."

"Something's wrong," Timon remarked firmly. "Professor wouldn't be gone this long without telling me, especially after what happened to Brian."

"It's not just you. I'm getting a bad feeling too," she informed him. "Asher had that look on his face when he left."

"Which look?"

"That all too familiar 'someone's going to die' look," she replied. "I need to use a computer, but I'm stuck here without a car. Is it possible for you to come and get me?"

"Uh, yeah, sure," Timon replied. "I can get the keys to Brian's Corvette. I always wanted to drive that car anyway. Give me fifteen minutes."

"Thanks, Timon."

Jacey replaced the phone to the cluttered desk then hurried from the study. She crossed the hall and entered Asher's bedroom, which remained dimly lit and the bed severely mussed. Jacey approached the closet, routed through it, and removed Asher's shoulder holster and gun from the box on the top shelf. She glanced in the closet at his leather jacket hanging before her. She tossed the shoulder holster onto the bed and grabbed Asher's jacket. Jacey stared at it a moment and sank into thought.

†

A few minutes had passed since Jacey hung up with Timon. She entered the sunroom now wearing Asher's leather jacket that had been hanging in the closet. She slipped into her shoes, where she had left them on the sunroom floor. They had been there since that morning before their erotic adventure. Something out of the corner of her eye caught her attention. She looked at the glass doors. One of the doors was partially open. Jacey stared at it a moment then nervously looked around the room.

"Shit."

She removed Asher's gun from the carefully hidden shoulder holster and slowly approached the glass door. She looked outside then shut and locked the door. After only a moment of debate, she headed for the doorway to the next room. Jacey cautiously entered the dimly lit front sitting room and looked around with her gun aimed. She'd search the house room by room. If someone broke into Asher's house, they wouldn't like the reception she was about to give them. The coat closet door near the foyer was partially open. Jacey slowly approached the closet door while keeping the gun trained on the opening. Someone appeared behind her in the dimly lit room. As she reached for the closet door, she was grabbed from behind and a cloth was placed over her mouth and nose. She gasped with surprise and immediately rammed her elbow backward, jabbing her attacker in the ribs. He released her while gasping with surprise to the sharp shot. She dropped to the floor and weakly reached for her discarded semiautomatic. The man sprang on top of her and once more applied the cloth to her nose and mouth. She barely struggled this time before collapsing to the floor.

Chapter Thirty-one

Nearly every light within the country club, both inside and out, was lit. Saturday nights were typically crowded at the club, being one of the few upscale places within a fifty-mile radius. In addition to the lounges and restaurants, there was usually some swank function being held in one or more of the banquet halls. Although, tonight's most talked about celebration was the bachelor party for the mayor's son. Just about anybody who was anybody from town and most of the county was invited. Asher's invitation probably got lost in the mail. Despite the expense and grandeur of the bachelor party, it would end as most did and the hangovers wouldn't discriminate. There were several dozen cars, which mostly filled the moderately small parking lot. Many cars, undoubtedly, would still be there in the morning.

Timon pulled up to the country club in Brian's borrowed, red Corvette. He got out of the sports car, seeing both Professor's sedan and Asher's SUV within the parking lot. Timon pressed the remote button to activate the car alarm, hearing the distinctive, electronic beep beep. He hurried to the front entrance of the country club and headed inside. Since it was a classy place, security usually consisted of men in expensive suits looking more like secret service than security guards. One neatly dressed guard casually monitored the main entrance, while a woman in a designer dress sat at the front desk looking like a cover model from a magazine. Her disinterest in working the desk was evident by the way she filed her nails. Timon approached the desk and flashed his membership card, although he'd met the woman in passing before. She barely acknowledged him and appeared annoyed that he interrupted her self-manicure.

"Hey, evening," Timon announced and attempted to act like a prestigious man with a degree for a change. He often came across like a country bumpkin rather than a man with a PhD. The receptionist typically looked down her nose at him as it was. "I was wondering if you could page either of my friends, Asher Konrad or Professor Ted Fuller."

She gave him an impatient look, maintaining a superior attitude. Despite Timon's PhD, she possibly was superior to him according to snob standards.

"Mr. Bennett--" she began in a scolding tone.

"Please, it's Timon," he interjected with a tiny grin, attempting to win her over.

She smirked in response, although it wasn't in a good way. "We don't page our members. If we did it for you, then we'd have to do it for everyone, and the board doesn't like the paging system. It interrupts our members' enjoyment."

"But this is important, Diane," Timon gently protested. "I can't find Professor anywhere and now Jacey seems to have disappeared as well." He placed his hands together and begged. "Please, make an exception just this once."

"It's Miss Hoffman," she scoffed with disinterest. "I'm sorry, Mr. Bennett, but the rules are the rules."

Timon was obviously displeased with her response and her snobbish tone. He casually placed his hands on the desk, leaned across it, and met her gaze. "That's *Doctor* Bennett to you," he snarled softly then straightened and walked away.

She stared after him with surprise, folded her arms across her chest, and then huffed in response.

†

Timon made his way around the entire country club, stopping in every lounge, restaurant, and even the private party in the smoking lounge looking for Asher, Professor, or Jacey. After nearly an hour, he'd have been happy to find Roxy or her father. He wasn't permitted to enter the smoking lounge due to the private bachelor party that he somehow wasn't invited to attend. It was moderately insulting, considering both Professor and Maxwell had been invited. Yet, somehow, he didn't rank. After scanning the smoke-filled lounge of nearly two hundred men puffing on cigars and drinking expensive cocktails served by scantily dressed cocktail waitresses, he finally gave up. When he caught a glimpse Sheriff Monroe among those in attendance, Timon frowned his annoyance. Even the sheriff ranked and everyone knew Sheriff Monroe and the mayor loathed each other.

Having searched all the most logical places, he started his quest in the less logical places. The kitchen was chaotic between the regular staff, caterers, and additional wait staff for the large bachelor party. The kitchen personnel weren't any more pleasant than the woman manning the front desk was or Lea at the smoking room entrance. After being chased from the kitchen, he entered the less traveled employees' corridor and saw someone who looked like Asher heading through a doorway at the far end of the hall.

"Asher!"

It was too late. The man was too far away to hear him. Timon hurried along the corridor at a walking jog. He stopped before the doorway Asher had passed through. It was marked laundry. Timon slowly pushed open the door and uncertainly entered the large, dimly lit laundry room with rolling bins, industrial sized washing machines, dryers, and presses. The laundry room was obviously closed for the night and appeared abandoned. There was no sign of the man who had passed through the doorway.

"Asher?" he called out while looking around. As he scanned the room, he rubbed his arms, apparently feeling a chill. He hadn't fared well in the laundry room at the museum gala just a few months ago. "This feels a little too familiar."

Timon remained near the open laundry room door and continued to scan the area now with increased anxiety. There were dark corners and creepy shadows every ten feet. He appeared moderately concerned, shook his head as if saying 'no way', and then turned in the doorway. He nearly collided with Davis, who was now standing behind him. Timon cried out and leaped backwards a step while clutching his chest. Davis jumped with surprise as well and stared at Timon. Both men took a moment to catch their breath then relaxed.

"Jesus, Timon," Davis gasped and released an uneasy laugh. "Don't do that."

"What the hell's wrong with you, sneaking up on me like that?" Timon demanded unable to remove his hand from his pounding heart.

"I wasn't sneaking," Davis insisted. "When I saw you come down here, I called but you must not have heard me. Why are you down here anyway? The bachelor party is upstairs." He then indicated the laundry room. "The laundry room is closed for the night."

"It's a long story, man," Timon informed him while shaking his head. "Everyone's vanishing around me. This town is like the Bermuda Triangle tonight."

"Tell me about it," Davis remarked with a soft groan. "I've been looking everywhere for Roxy. She came here with me this morning, but I haven't seen her since. She couldn't have left. I mean, she could have gotten a ride from someone, but she wouldn't just leave without telling me first. It's important I locate her. I'm getting worried."

Timon looked concerned as he stared at Davis. "Professor left a note saying he was meeting Roxy for lunch this afternoon," Timon insisted. "His car is here--but no Professor. No one's seen him either. A tall guy like that is hard to miss." His concerned look increased. "Then Jacey calls me and asks me to pick her up at Asher's place, because she didn't have a car. When I got there, she was gone."

"Her jeep is here."

"That's because she left it here last night when she drove Asher home. They took his car," he informed Davis. Timon's eyes then lit up. "Hey, why don't we look for them together? You know, safety in numbers. I mean, they're probably all hanging out somewhere and forgot to tell us."

"That's a good idea," Davis replied. "I haven't checked the indoor pool. Even though it's closed, they could be there. I didn't look in the steam room and spa areas either."

"I didn't think to look in those areas either," Timon announced and attempted to relax. "Maybe they're having a party and forgot to invite us."

†

Timon and Davis entered the large, enclosed pool and spa area. There were several doors leading to both the men and women's locker rooms, massage areas, segregated steam rooms, and the unisex weight room. Despite climate control, the large pool area was moderately moist and smelled heavily of chlorine. Both walked around the large, elegant pool. The area was an endless circle of corridors, doorways and rooms, allowing guests to move freely from one area to the next without changing out of swimsuits and plush, country club robes.

"Things have been very strange around here tonight," Davis remarked to Timon. "Carl and Nathan seemed pretty tense at our dinner meeting."

"After what happened to Brian, I'm not surprised," Timon replied. "Monroe seems to suspect everyone."

"Nathan thinks it was Asher," Davis announced while briefly glancing at him.

"That would certainly solve all his problems, wouldn't it?" Timon muttered. "I heard Brian had brought up the proposal of bringing Asher on as an investor and board member. Must really have burned Nathan's britches."

"After he was exonerated of the institute fire three months ago, I've been on Asher's side with all the town drama," Davis informed him. "Now, I'm not so sure I want to be associated with him."

Timon glanced at him with surprise. "What? Why's that?" he asked.

"Several club members are being blackmailed," Davis reluctantly informed him. "When the blackmail photos and notes arrive, they're always on days Asher visits the club. They contain postage but none are cancelled, which means someone is tossing them into the exterior mail bin." He hesitated. "There are just little things that keep pointing to him, and I can't turn a blind eye to it much longer."

"Asher? A blackmailer?" Timon suddenly asked. He snorted a soft laugh. "That's not Asher's style. He's also not a killer." Timon then hesitated and appeared to reconsider. "I mean, he'd never murder anyone."

Timon approached the steam room door and peered inside. Davis paused before the men's locker room and pushed the door open.

"I'd like to believe you're right," Davis announced then sighed. "Roxy, on the other hand, is very leery of Asher. Might be my fault, I suppose. When he was first branded a killer all those years ago, I was quick to jump on the bandwagon with the rest of the town. Roxy was a very impressionable little girl, and I may have frightened her with the institute stories. She saw him as a monster after that."

While looking into the locker room, Davis appeared curious and stepped inside. The door shut behind him. Timon stood across the corridor while peering into the sauna room then stepped out and closed the door.

"I suppose that's natural--" Timon turned and realized Davis was no longer with him. He looked around with increased concern. "Davis?"

When there was no response, he moved from door-to-door and looked into each room. He opened the men's locker room door as well and peered inside.

"Davis!"

There was still no response. Timon shut the door and hurried to the nearby women's locker room. He vigorously opened the door and looked inside.

"Davis, where are you?" he demanded, although his fears were getting the better of him. He shut the door and looked around. "Shit, not again." Timon hurried back toward the main door by the indoor pool.

Chapter Thirty-two

Soft female moans were heard from within the dark reception office. The faint sound of something scraping the floor coincided with the moans, lending an eeriness to the darkened room. A male silhouette appeared just outside the frosted reception office door in the dimly lit corridor. There was a soft click from the door as the lock was manipulated. The main door slowly opened and someone slipped inside the darkened reception area. There was another female moan. The light suddenly came on. Carl had Angel bent forward over Jacey's desk in a compromising position while he held her hips from behind, thrusting wildly, his pants on the floor around his ankles. Both appeared startled, stopped what they were doing, and looked at the open door.

Asher casually stood inside the door with his hand on the light switch. Carl quickly pulled away from Angel, almost knocking her to the floor as he dove behind the desk. Angel allowed her skirt to fall back into place as she straightened and casually buttoned her shirt, covering her exposed bra. Her tiny grin indicated she wasn't ashamed that she'd been caught in the act with one of the board members. Carl poked his head up from behind the desk and nervously chuckled while obviously pulling up his pants.

"Asher, what brings you by here so late?" he gasped, attempting to act as if nothing had happened.

Asher didn't even react to what he had just witnessed. His expression remained disinterested. "I'm looking for Professor," he announced with little emotion. "Have you seen him?"

Carl stood and tucked in his shirt while Angel adjusted her short skirt. Whether or not she wore underwear was officially up for debate.

"Uh, Professor," he remarked and appeared to give the question some consideration, but it was obvious he was distracted about being caught banging the attractive bartender. "Uh, actually, I haven't seen him."

"I'm sure you haven't," Asher remarked.

Angel slipped into her daringly high stiletto heels and glanced at Carl.

"Times up, Carl," she announced. "I'll be sure to add my tip to your tab."

Angel then headed toward Asher and the door without further comment. She smiled and winked at Asher. He barely acknowledged her as she walked past him and out the door.

"What about Roxy? Have you seen her?" Asher demanded, becoming impatient, not giving a damn that he ruined Carl's expensive romp.

"Roxy?" Carl announced with surprise and attempted to act casual by sitting on the edge of the desk. He immediately fidgeted, wiped his hand on his pants, and straightened. "Why are you looking for Roxy?"

Asher eyed Carl's hand then the spot he'd left behind on his pants but didn't comment on it. Carl again fidgeted and fumbled for anything to say to break Asher's fixed stare upon him.

"Oh, uh, good news. The board voted tonight," Carl announced while attempting a smile and appeared enthusiastic. "You're in."

"Uh, huh," Asher remarked with disinterest. "Well, I'm withdrawing my proposal and revoking my membership. You can keep the remaining yearly dues."

Carl's expression suddenly dropped, being stunned by the news. "But it's been voted on. You're in," he announced with more conviction. "What about the club and Jacey?"

"Jacey doesn't work here anymore," Asher replied with little emotion. "She's accepted another position."

Without further comment, Asher turned and left the office, shutting the door behind him. Carl frowned then slammed his fist on the computer monitor.

"Son-of-a-bitch!"

Carl turned and stormed into Nathan's darkened office. He flipped on the light, crossed the room, and collapsed into the swivel chair behind the desk. He snatched the phone from its cradle and pressed a button.

When the call was answered, he grumbled into the phone, "He backed out." Carl listened to the person on the other end then became irritated. "Konrad Asher! Who the hell do you think?" He fell silent and listened another moment while frowning. "That's what I thought too."

The lights went out leaving Carl in the dark. He sat forward from behind Nathan's desk and looked around in total darkness.

"Hello?" he said into the phone, but there was no sound.

Carl cursed and returned the phone to its cradle. He felt for the computer mouse and rolled it. The computer monitor lit up, giving the room a faint glow. He looked around the empty office then stood and approached the door. As he passed through the doorway, he looked across the nearly dark reception area to the fuse box on the wall just beyond Jeannette's desk. To his surprise, the fuse box door was hanging open. He stopped his approach and again looked around the darkened room. Carl appeared concerned and quickly turned back for Nathan's office. As he entered the office, someone lunged out of the darkness from behind Jeannette's desk and tackled him to the floor. Carl screamed and struggled against his attacker, but the smaller man was no match for his assailant. The assailant held him pinned to the floor with his knee in his abdomen and his hand to his throat. The blade of a knife glistened off the glow of the computer monitor, allowing Carl to see the weapon just before it was thrust downward into his upper chest. The knife was pulled back several times, repeatedly stabbing him as blood spattered off the blade.

✝

Twenty minutes later, Sheriff Monroe, dressed in his finest cheap suit, walked along the back corridor while looking around. He approached the reception office, noting the open door and the darkness beyond it. The door should have been shut and locked. As Sheriff Monroe approached the doorway, a large man darted from the darkness of the reception area and collided with the sheriff. Both men crashed to the floor. Timon quickly scrambled to his feet and stared at Sheriff Monroe. As he sat up, Monroe saw the blood on Timon's hands and the horrified look on his face.

"Monroe," Timon cried out with panic and pointed his bloodied finger to the dark reception office. "It's Carl! Someone killed him!"

Monroe appeared alarmed, scrambled to his feet, and removed his hidden revolver from his belt holster. Monroe cautiously entered the reception area with Timon directly on his heels. The glow from the Nathan's computer was just bright enough to reveal Carl's outstretched hand within the open doorway and the quickly collecting pool of blood beneath him. Monroe flipped the light switch by the main door, but the light didn't come on. He turned to Timon with a concerned look on his face. Neither was ready for a repeat of the museum gala massacre.

"Call the station for additional backup," Monroe ordered while clutching his gun.

"I tried," Timon announced and indicated Jacey's desk. "The phones don't work either. Someone messed with the fuse box on the wall over there." He indicated the open fuse box across the room. "When the power goes out, network phones won't work. Only equipment plugged into emergency outlets work off the generator, which is usually reserved for computers."

Sheriff Monroe eyed him suspiciously. "You seem to know an awful lot about power outages."

"Yeah, there was another incident very similar to this one," Timon snarled at the sheriff.

"There's a phone just around the corner in the hall," Monroe informed him while giving a general nod toward the office door. "Try that one. If you can't get a dial tone, go to the smoking room. Someone in there will have a cell phone."

Timon uncertainly nodded then hurried from the room. Monroe slowly entered the reception office. He approached Nathan's office and got his first look at Carl's body just beyond the doorway, finally able to identify him. Monroe replaced his gun to his hidden holster, crouched before the dead man, and observed the multiple stab wounds along with the blood spatter from the gruesome kill.

"Jesus--" he muttered.

Monroe appeared alerted to someone's presence and was about to turn while reaching for his hidden gun when he was suddenly struck on the head. Monroe half stood, staggered away from the doorway, and then fell to the floor. Sheriff Monroe was grabbed by the ankles and pulled across the dark room.

Chapter Thirty-three

Jacey slowly woke from where she lie face down on an old, hardwood floor. She sat up, feeling disoriented, and her head pounded. As she gingerly touched her head, she felt a comforting hand touch her shoulder. She looked up and saw Professor kneeling over her. He gently touched her face with a sympathetic look and offered a tiny smile. Jacey was so relieved to see Professor; she barely noticed the dried blood in his hairline. She threw her arms around his neck and hugged him. He returned the embrace. She pulled back and looked at him with relief.

"Oh, Professor," she gasped softly. "Thank God you're okay. We thought something terrible happened to you."

Professor dabbed the dried blood near the back of his head and forced a tiny smile. "You're not far off with that," he remarked gently.

She stared at the dried blood and became concerned. "Oh, are you okay?"

"How I'm feeling is the least of our worries," he replied.

Jacey uncertainly looked around and realized she was in the last aisle of the file room. Horror shuttered through her body as she took in her surroundings.

"How the hell did I get here?" she gasped.

Jacey then saw Roxy pacing at the end of aisle, her arms folded across her chest and a frightened look on her youthful face. She looked demandingly at Jacey and Professor where they remained on the floor.

"Are you going to tell her or should I?" Roxy growled impatiently.

Jacey looked from Roxy to Professor with panic in her eyes. "Tell me what? What's going on?"

"We're all sort of trapped down here," Professor informed her then inhaled deeply and seemed reluctant to continue. He stared into her eyes with increasing concern for their situation. "Roxy found evidence that suggests Jeanette and Brian may have been blackmailing Asher."

"May have?" Roxy demanded then groaned with disgust and returned to pacing.

Jacey stared at Professor with a shocked look. She attempted to pull herself to her feet, although her head was still spinning slightly from the drugs used to knock her out.

"Asher didn't kill Jeanette or Brian," Jacey announced bluntly. "Everyone in town has threatened or attempted to blackmail Asher at one time or another. It's common knowledge. He's the perfect scapegoat for all occasions."

"Well, this could be a little different. Roxy found one of those spy cam pens in Jeanette's desk," Professor gently informed her. "When she inserted the USB into the computer, it pulled up video of a heated argument between Brian and Asher."

"Involving you," Roxy bluntly informed Jacey.

Jacey stared at Roxy a moment then glanced at Professor. "Not exactly news. That's not really anything new," she remarked. "It certainly wouldn't prove he killed Brian."

"But it gives him motive," Roxy informed her, becoming disgusted with the entire Asher debate. "Brian was using an argument he'd heard between Asher and Maxwell against Asher. Brian wanted Asher to become a board member, so he'd vote with him and Carl."

Professor appeared sympathetic while watching Jacey process the information. "I would appear Asher and Maxwell got into an altercation--over you. Asher admitted he was in love with you, which is around the same time things went south between them." He gently took her hand and stared into her eyes. "You said Asher was acting strangely. With what Jeannette and Brian were holding over him, that was probably why he was behaving that way."

Jacey gently placed her hand over Professor's and stared back into his eyes with a serious look. Her words were calm but bitter. "Are you actually suggesting Asher abducted and dumped me here? Do you know how insane that sounds?"

"Stop defending the guy," Roxy blurted out. "Your blind faith in the guy is going to get you killed. Maybe us too!" She took a deep breath and attempted to remain calm. "Someone knocked both of us out," Roxy informed her. "Neither of us saw who did it, but we can't rule out Asher."

Jacey rolled her eyes and was about to defend Asher when Roxy continued with her rant.

"The two of us were blindfolded, tied, and gagged here in the file room," she announced firmly. "We're not sure how long we were being held. In fact, we didn't even know the other was down here until a few minutes ago."

"After we heard someone enter the file room, presumably dumping you, we managed to get untied," Professor informed her. "That's when we found you."

"I know you care about Asher, Jacey," Roxy announced with a more sympathetic tone, "but you have to see it all points back to him."

"It always points to him," Jacey snapped. "And they've never been right. I was with Asher all afternoon. He certainly didn't sneak out and abduct the two of you. I assure you, he never left his cabin." There was no doubt. She could vouch that he'd never even left his bed, but she didn't want to announce that.

"He's crafty," Roxy replied. "I'm sure you weren't with him the whole time."

Asher was indeed crafty, but she also knew his craftiness this afternoon was all about seeing how many positions he could safely attempt without causing physical harm to either of them. Jacey wasn't going to have the Asher argument with Roxy. She knew she'd never convince her of Asher's innocence even if she admitted to her afternoon of passion with the town's most infamous man. What she did find troublesome was Professor actually buying into Roxy's story. He knew Asher better than to believe any wild rumors.

"After what happened last night, he could have gone over the deep end," Professor gently informed her.

Now he was just pissing her off. She decided against sharing how she knew Asher was innocent.

"He didn't go over the deep end," Jacey insisted to Professor. "He was with me all afternoon. You're just going to have to trust me on this. He's your friend, Professor, you know him better than that."

"He's on the edge and has nothing left to lose," Roxy insisted. "I saw him last night when he was drunk--or I should say pretending to be drunk."

Jacey appeared surprised then angered.

"He was afraid he'd lose you and he blamed the board members and those who were blackmailing him," Roxy informed her. "I know how men like that think. You're not above his wrath. If he can't have you, he'll see you dead. Who else could it be? Who else had reason to abduct you?"

She sharply eyed the young woman she thought was her friend. If Roxy thought Asher was the killer type because he was protective of her, she'd be in for a rude awakening when she realized Jacey was twice as protective of Asher. She'd probably realize it when Jacey finally punched her in the face.

"I'm guessing anyone with an ax to grind against Asher, would be a good start," Jacey snapped while staring at Roxy. "I can easily blow your entire theory out of the water, but we'll have to save that debate for later. We should get out of here before whoever left us here comes back to carry out their plan." Jacey looked around for a possible escape.

"Don't bother," Roxy informed her with a slight hiss in her tone, further agitated by her co-worker. "The door has been locked from the outside and no one will hear us scream in this remote corner of the building."

"Then we'll just go out the back door," Jacey informed her, attempting to keep her temper from rising.

Both looked at Jacey with surprise as she left the aisle. Professor and Roxy hurried after her. Jacey approached the opposite end of the room and removed boxes from a steel frame shelf. Once the boxes were removed, they could see an old door hidden behind the shelf. Jacey unbolted the door and pushed it open to reveal a dark staircase climbing upward. She looked back at them.

"This used to be the wine cellar, remember?" she informed them then indicated the dark opening. "They blocked off the stairs leading up to the kitchen years ago. This will take us to the back of the kitchen."

Professor glanced at the large doorway reduced to a crawl space by the position of the heavy shelf. He looked back at them with moderate concern.

"I'd better go first. In case I get stuck, you can push," Professor remarked timidly.

"Yeah, and chase the spiders away while you're at it," Roxy muttered.

Professor eyed her and frowned with distaste. "Spiders, yuk."

Jacey watched as Professor then Roxy crawled through the small opening and into the darkened stairs where they could finally stand. Jacey reached down the front of her shirt and removed the flash drive to make sure it was still there. Whoever abducted her had no idea she had it on her, so they didn't grab her to get their hands on the device. She needed to find out what was on the flash drive, but she'd need access to a computer first. She returned the flash drive down the front of her shirt for safekeeping. Jacey knew she'd have to view it in private first to avoid doctored evidence against Asher falling into the wrong hands. She crawled beneath the shelf and into the small opening behind the others.

Chapter Thirty-four

The room was completely black. A loud crack broke the silence. Professor stepped through the broken door of the dark, secret passageway into an equally dark room. He attempted to look around, although there was nothing to see. Jacey and Roxy appeared behind him in the darkness. Both women collided into him, unaware that he had stopped.

"Where are we? Why is it so dark?" Roxy asked while feeling around the room.

"We're in the pantry," Jacey explained. "The pantry was built after the country club bought the place."

"How do you know so much about this place?" Professor asked while feeling around in the dark. "I thought the club was only a few years old."

"No. Before it was a country club, it was a summer mansion belonging to some politician," Jacey replied and fumbled across the dark pantry, bumping into Professor as she felt her way to the door. "When I was a little girl, my father did some remodeling for them. Since the owner's didn't want to stay here during the renovations, I hung out with my father and explored the mansion for the three weeks he worked on the place."

Jacey reached the wall and felt for the light switch. The light came on and brightened the pantry. The pantry was huge and held many shelves containing food supplies and various other kitchen items. Roxy appeared uncomfortable while looking around and rubbing her arms.

"Can we just get out of here?" Roxy almost demanded.

Jacey opened the pantry door and nearly collided with Timon, who was about to open the door from the outside. Both jumped back from each other and screamed. After taking a moment to recover, Jacey entered the kitchen from the pantry and hugged Timon. He half-heartedly returned the embrace then looked at Professor and Roxy as they joined him in the kitchen.

"What the hell--?" Timon cried out then studied all three. "What were you doing hanging out in the kitchen pantry?"

"It's a long story," Professor replied. "We need to call Sheriff Monroe."

"That's another long story," Timon muttered.

"What do you mean?" Jacey demanded.

Timon became animated by the question, and he started gesturing wildly with his hands. "What do I mean? I mean, everyone is disappearing around here," he loudly voiced his concern. "I've been losing everyone. They're here one minute and then gone the next." He then hesitated and appeared reluctant to speak. "Then there's Carl--"

"What's wrong with Carl?" Professor asked.

"He's dead," Timon exploded with horror. "Someone killed him!"

Roxy gasped and placed her hand to her mouth.

Timon attempted to relax and remain calm, but he was having a difficult time. "Monroe was in the office with Carl's body, and I went to call for his backup, but it seems there isn't a single working phone in this dump," he explained. "When I went back, Monroe was gone too." Timon then turned hostile and pointed from the kitchen. "And that little twit guarding the bachelor party won't let me in to find someone with a cell phone." He hesitated only long enough to take a deep breath. "I was going to drive to the police station, but that's when I heard you thumping around in the pantry." He then looked at Professor and appeared enthusiastic. "You were invited to the bachelor party. They'll let you in. You can find someone with a cell phone."

The thought of Carl being dead and Sheriff Monroe vanishing had Jacey concerned for many reasons, but one weighed heavily on her mind.

"Have you seen Asher?" Jacey asked Timon.

"Yeah, a while ago. At least I think it was him," Timon remarked, although he seemed uncertain. "I only saw him from the back. I called to him, but I guess he didn't hear me. I followed him, but then he disappeared too. I'm telling you, *everyone* has vanished."

"Timon's right," Jacey announced to Professor. "You should go to the smoking lounge, borrow someone's cell phone, and call the police. Sheriff Monroe wouldn't just leave a crime scene without good reason." She fidgeted slightly. "I have to find Asher."

Jacey received stares from all three. She glared at them then looked away with annoyance. "And don't you guys give me that look," she snarled. "I know what I'm doing."

"Then I'm going with you," Timon announced.

Professor glared at Timon with a look of disbelief or possible annoyance. Timon glared back at him and appeared insulted from the look he'd received.

"I know what I'm doing too," Timon insisted.

"You're both insane," Professor scoffed.

Professor motioned for Roxy to follow him. Both headed across the kitchen. Jacey looked at Timon and attempted a weak smile. She was grateful for the moral support as well as someone covering her back.

"Thanks, Timon."

"Yeah, well, I'm just going along to make sure you don't disappear too," he muttered then shook his head. "This shit is seriously freaking me out."

†

Roxy and Professor stood within the doorway to the smoking lounge and stared into the room with disbelief. The entire room was empty. Everyone was gone! It seemed Timon wasn't kidding. Everyone was disappearing! They looked at each other with a shared look of confusion.

"What's going on around here?" Roxy suddenly demanded. "Where is everyone?"

"It's not even ten o'clock," Professor remarked. "The party couldn't have broken up this early."

They uncertainly entered the lounge and looked around. It seemed as if everyone left rather suddenly, although not in a 'fleeing for their lives' sort of way. There were glasses of beer and mixed drinks on the tables as well as lining the bar. Cigars were partially crushed yet still smoldering in the ashtrays, and trays of appetizers were carelessly setting on tables. Both scanned the room as they crossed it. Roxy clung to Professor's arm while apprehensive about the appearance of the lounge.

"I don't like this," Roxy muttered softly.

Professor gently pulled free from her grip, approached the bar, and looked behind it. Angel suddenly straightened from behind the bar, startling Professor. Both Angel and Professor cried out with surprise. Angel had a handful of cash and the register remained open. She easily closed the register with her hip and attempted a smile while slipping the money in her apron pocket.

"What are you guys doing here?" she asked while lightly fidgeting. "I thought everyone had left." She then looked at Roxy. "Your father was looking for you, Roxy."

"Where did everyone go?" Professor asked while looking around the eerily silent room then met her gaze with distrust. "What's going on around here?"

"Where have you guys been? The fire alarm went off nearly thirty minutes ago," Angel informed them. "Everyone's outside in the front parking lot waiting for the fire department."

"Fire alarm? No, we didn't hear the fire alarm," Roxy replied and appeared curious as she cast a glance at Professor.

The file room was moderately soundproof, so it was possible they didn't hear it. Professor didn't comment, but his look matched Roxy's expression.

"Eh, it's probably just another false alarm anyway. We've been having some trouble with the alarms the past few weeks," Angel informed them. "We should probably wait in the parking lot with the others."

Angel rounded the bar, casually walked past them, and left the lounge. Roxy and Professor watched her leave then looked at one another.

"Why didn't Timon mention the fire alarm?" Roxy questioned.

"I think we'd better find Jacey and get the hell out of here," Professor announced with concern. "This is starting to feel too much like old times."

Professor took Roxy's hand and led her toward the lounge doorway. Roxy suddenly stopped him. He turned to face her with some surprise. She appeared concerned.

"It's not a good idea to go after Jacey," Roxy remarked. "If she's found Asher--"

"She's my friend," Professor insisted, almost disbelieving what he was hearing. "I can't just leave her wandering around this place. It smells of a setup."

"And Konrad Asher is behind it," Roxy firmly insisted, becoming defensive again.

"We don't know that," Professor protested. "Even he has more imagination then that. This is too much like 'museum gala revisited' for my liking." He vigorously shook his head. "I think someone is trying to imitate the museum gala in order to frame Asher." He fidgeted with concern. "I suddenly have a really bad feeling."

Professor tugged on her hand and attempted to pull her from the smoking lounge behind him. Professor's body suddenly jerked, and he collapsed to the floor, twitching slightly. Roxy flashed the stun gun along with a tiny smile, although Professor was in no condition to notice her.

"I don't think you'll be saying anything to Jacey," Roxy remarked. "It would ruin my perfect plan, Professor. I'm really sorry I involved you, but it was necessary."

Chapter Thirty-five

Jacey and Timon walked along the quiet hallway toward the back of the country club. Both glanced around with shared looks of concern.

"It's awfully quiet around here, don't you think?" Timon remarked.

"Where is everyone?"

"Probably fell through a black hole or something," Timon muttered. "The fire alarm went off half an hour ago, but it stopped after only a minute. I sort of doubt they evacuated the place because of a false alarm."

Jacey suddenly stopped and turned to face him with a suspicious look.

He stared at her with concern. "Did I say something wrong?"

"I overheard Nathan telling Davis they couldn't shut off the security cameras, because it would trip the fire alarm since they were on the same line," she informed him then sank into thought.

"Do you think the fire alarm went off because someone shut off the security cameras?"

"If you wanted to murder someone, it would help to shut off video of you committing the crime," she informed him then shook her head. "I have this terrible feeling someone is setting up Asher to take the fall."

"What should we do?" Timon asked with concern.

"I need to find Asher," she announced. "You need to call the police and get some officers out here in case Professor was unsuccessful finding a cell phone."

"Back to my original plan," he remarked. "I'll drive to town and get the police myself." Timon appeared concerned while studying her. "Although, I don't know that I should leave you alone here. Asher can take care of himself. You should probably come with me."

"Asher handling himself isn't the problem," she informed Timon. "It's someone attempting to frame him that worries me. I need to prevent that from happening."

"Do you know who the killer is, Jacey?" Timon asked. "If you do, tell me."

She shook her head. "There's the usual list of suspects, but I really couldn't say." Jacey removed the flash drive from her cleavage. "But I have a feeling this may have some answers. I need to access a computer. I'm pretty sure the 'why' is to cover up Carl's murder and a far-reaching blackmail scheme."

"Then we should get you and that thumb drive out of here," he announced with panic in his voice.

"You just worry about the getting the police out here," she informed him and returned the flash drive down the front of her shirt. "I need to find Asher before someone else does."

Jacey turned and ran down the hall. Timon helplessly stared after her.

"No, Jacey! Wait! Jacey," he called after her then groaned with disgust. "Come back!"

Timon nervously fidgeted while running his fingers through his hair, considered his options, and then hurried toward the smoking lounge and a possible cell phone. As he headed toward the main corridor, he nearly collided with Angel. Both jumped with surprise then relaxed.

"What are you still doing in the building?" Angel asked sternly.

"What do you mean?"

"Everyone's supposed to stay outside until the fire department arrives and announces it's okay to return inside," she replied matter-of-fact.

"You mean there isn't anyone in the smoking lounge?" he asked with concern.

"No," she replied. "Everyone is out front. I'm sure they took the party with them. I saw a few of the guys smuggling some bottles of booze out of the lounge when they left."

"So anyone with a cell phone is outside?"

"I would assume so," Angel replied.

"Could you do me a favor?"

She shrugged and grinned. "Sure, what's the favor?"

†

Jacey hurried into the darkened reception office and tried the lights. To her surprise, they didn't work. She approached her desk, which was only visible from the glow of Nathan's office, and rolled her mouse across the pad. The glow from her computer monitor brightened the reception area just enough. She saw a man's pale hand sticking out of Nathan's office doorway. Jacey approached the open doorway and stopped as soon as she saw Carl's lifeless body lying in a pool of blood just inside the office. Blood was spattered along a large portion of the carpet. Despite having heard about Carl's murder, she still wasn't prepared for the gruesomeness of the crime scene. Jacey backed away from the dead man, returned to her desk while removing the flash drive from her cleavage, and inserted it into the USB port. She collapsed into her chair and opened one of three files on the flash drive.

Jacey scanned through nearly one hundred different photos of her bosses as well as other club members. Every photo appeared to be taken using some sort of spy camera. Some were fairly old, relatively grainy, and mostly black and white. Each picture had one common theme. Club members behaving badly, badly enough that the mere sight of the pictures would be enough to warrant a payoff to whomever possessed them. Jacey quickly skimmed the photos and saw many of members with women who clearly weren't their wives. She recognized some of the women as club employees. Most of the photos were X-rated in nature. The second file contained grainy video footage, possibly recorded within the last year or two. Most were pornographic, again involving some of the same men seen in the photos. One thumbnail in particular caught her interest. She could clearly make out Maxwell and Asher in the museum's game room, which was shot from behind a doorframe. She played the video and nervously chewed on her fingernail. Jacey was slightly unnerved to what she'd discover about the man she loved. The video played on her computer monitor.

"*I know what you're up to, Asher,*" Maxwell snarled at him. "*You're in love with Jacey. Don't bother to deny it.*"

"*Jacey's my friend,*" Asher scoffed. "*There's nothing inappropriate between us, and I'll ask you only once to keep your accusations to yourself.*"

Maxell suddenly laughed then glared at Asher. "*Nothing inappropriate? That's a good one!*" His look turned hateful and angry. "*You're the reason I can't even get to second base with Jacey.*"

"*That's the most ridiculous comment I've ever heard,*" Asher snapped back and became angry. "*If you can't get to second base with her, it's probably because you're behaving like this.*"

"*My behavior isn't the issue,*" Maxwell lashed out. "*It's your behavior that's the distraction. You're always holding her and kissing her as if you're her lover. That's not how friends behave together.*"

"*That's how our friendship works,*" Asher casually replied. "*If you have a problem with it, take it up with Jacey.*"

"*A little hard to do when you always have your hands on my girlfriend,*" Maxwell launched back. "*Just admit it. You want to fuck Jacey.*"

Asher stood perfectly still while staring at Maxwell. The look on Maxwell's face suddenly turned to horror, as he must have realized what he'd said. Without warning, Asher swept Maxwell's legs out beneath him, dropping him to the floor on his backside. Asher pounced on top of him, pressing his knee into Maxwell's chest, and clutched his throat in his hand. Asher's expression never changed as he glared at the gasping man beneath him.

"*You better fucking believe I love Jacey,*" Asher casually snarled. "*I've loved her longer and deeper than you ever could. If you ever disrespect her like that again, I'll happily tear out your throat.*" Asher smirked in a sinister manner. "*Are we clear on that?*"

Maxwell gasped and managed a slight nod. Asher released him and sprang back to his feet. He straightened his jacket, offered a pleasant smile, and walked away, leaving Maxwell half sitting up, clutching his throat, and gasping. While someone continued to record, Brain rushed into the room and assisted Maxwell. As Asher approached the doorway and the camera, the video abruptly ended.

Jacey leaned back in her chair while holding her breath. "Well, that explains why Asher put some distance between us," she muttered.

172

Jacey eyed the thumbnails a little closer, appeared curious, and pressed the next one. She watched the pornographic video clearly taken from a strategically placed spy camera. Jeannette was seen receiving oral sex by someone in the video, although it was hard to tell who she was in bed with. The video was date stamped, taken almost two weeks prior to the museum fundraiser. Despite wanting to stop the video, she allowed it to play. She wanted to satisfy her curiosity about Jeannette and Nathan, especially since it proved they were having an affair prior to Doyle's death. The person on the bottom edge of the video straightened and moved closer to Jeannette to kiss her. Jacey stared with surprise at Roxy as she kissed Jeannette.

"Roxy?" Jacey gasped softly.

She paused the video and stared at the image of Roxy with Jeannette, detailing their affair. Jacey sank into thought. The video was obviously recorded without either woman's knowledge. The angle was horrible, indicating neither woman attempted to keep the other within the frame. That had to mean the video was crudely set up and taken by a third-party. Jacey considered the situation a moment then came to only one conclusion. Doyle set up the camera to catch his wife having an affair! By the age of some of the photos and videos, he was probably behind most of the collected blackmail. Was Doyle blackmailing his fellow board members and club buddies? But that didn't explain Asher and Brian. Doyle was dead long before that fight would have taken place. Obviously, it wasn't Brian doing the recording of Asher and Maxwell. Brian had also mentioned someone attempting to blackmail him as well. She considered all the evidence a moment longer then came to a startling conclusion. Roxy recorded the fight between Asher and Maxwell! She started dating Brian shortly after the museum fundraiser. She could have been at the museum and witnessed the fight!

Jacey suddenly had to ask herself if Doyle's death was really a murder suicide, or was it actually a double homicide? It was almost too much information for her to process at once. Then the envelope popped into her head. The flash drive had been mailed to Asher written in Jeannette's handwriting. Why would Jeannette mail proof of blackmail to Asher? She certainly wasn't blackmailing him. The incident in the video wasn't damning enough. Why send him proof that her husband had blackmailed others at the club? Wouldn't she realize Asher would turn it over to Sheriff Monroe? Then it dawned on her. Jeannette called her right before she was murdered claiming to have urgent information regarding Asher. Jeannette *wanted* the information turned over to the police! She must have known someone was after her and realized she could count on Asher to do anything in his power to destroy the country club. If Sheriff Monroe was intimidated to act because of those involved, she knew Asher would make sure it got out. A few things didn't make any sense though. Roxy didn't kill Jeannette. She ran into the killer at Jeannette's house. He was definitely male. The facts didn't add up in her mind.

Davis staggered into the reception office doorway while clutching his bleeding temple. His presence startled Jacey, causing her to eject the flash drive hastily from the computer. When she realized Davis had been injured, she shot up from her chair. Davis appeared to be in bad shape and obviously had a run-in with the killer himself. He appeared equally surprised to see her as well then appeared relieved.

"Oh, Jacey," he gasped softly and lowered his bloodied hand from his head. "Thank God I found someone. The entire club is abandoned. I don't know what happened."

While Davis was busy looking at the blood on his hand, Jacey slipped the flash drive down her shirt. She hurried around her desk toward him where he remained in the doorway. She visually assessed his bleeding temple. He'd sustained a hard hit with fresh blood running freely from the wound and down his sideburns to his neck. Davis' look suddenly froze as he stared past her at the exposed dead man's hand and traces of blood outside Nathan's office.

"My God, Carl," Davis suddenly gasped.

Jacey glanced back at the office doorway then met Davis' transfixed gaze and the horror in his eyes. Her mind was now reeling.

"We need to get you out of here," she insisted then twitched with concern. "Something bad is about to happen."

"Not without my daughter," he launched back. "I've been looking for her all evening, but she's gone. Something's happened to her, I know it."

"Roxy's fine," Jacey informed him. "She went with Professor to get help."

"What's going on, Jacey?" he suddenly demanded. "What happened to Carl? Where is everyone?"

Jacey stared at him a moment, took a deep breath, and attempted to remain calm. "I have reason to believe someone intends to frame Asher for Carl's murder," she replied.

Davis was stunned. "What? Who?"

She hesitated and gently rubbed her chilled shoulders. "If I'm correct, Nathan's behind this."

"Nathan?" he suddenly gasped. "That can't be."

"Have you seen him tonight?" she questioned with an accusing, raised brow.

Davis then hesitated and sank into thought. He gave Jacey an odd stare. "As a matter-of-fact, I did," he suddenly gasped. "I saw him heading for the file room stairs as I was approaching the office. I called to him, but he didn't hear me."

"The file room, of course," she replied. "That makes sense. He's expecting to find a few hostages down there." She looked back at Davis. "I have to go after him."

"What? No!" Davis shook his head then immediately regretted the action and clutched his head. "If Nathan's a killer, he won't hesitate to take you out, Jacey. Leave it to the police."

"You don't understand," Jacey announced with concern. "If he is behind this, the only way to get away with it would be to burn the place down. A fire in the file room would spread rapidly. That place will go up in a matter of minutes, destroying this area and all evidence of Carl's murder."

"You can't go after him alone," Davis insisted and boldly straightened. "I'm going with you."

She nodded. "I thought you might."

Chapter Thirty-six

Jacey and Davis cautiously walked down the stairs to the basement file room with Davis in the lead. As they approached the bottom of the stairs, they saw Nathan lying on the floor with blood surrounding his head. Jacey hurried past Davis to Nathan's motionless body and checked for a pulse, even though she was almost certain of his condition. Asher appeared from the end aisle with his gun aimed at them. Jacey jumped with surprise and quickly straightened. Asher gave her a bewildered look and slowly lowered his gun.

"Jacey, what are you doing here?" Asher almost demanded, clearly surprised to see her.

"Flushing out a killer," she casually replied.

Asher's expression hardened as he aimed his gun at them. Jacey's showed little reaction as she turned toward Davis behind her and saw the gun he aimed at her head. It was the same gun taken off her at Asher's cabin. She eyed the familiar gun then her boss. He frowned with annoyance and appeared almost saddened by the outcome.

"It wasn't supposed to happen this way," he gently informed her. "It's nothing personal, Jacey."

She frowned and folded her arms across her chest. "It never is." Jacey shook her head while studying him. "Award-winning performance on showing surprise to Carl's murder. Unfortunately, you wouldn't have known it was Carl's body from where you were standing. Since it was Nathan's office, you should have assumed it was Nathan who was dead."

"Pretty stupid," Davis muttered.

"You never were good at bluffing," Asher muttered.

Davis frowned while staring at Jacey. "I didn't want to involve you," he announced.

"Then why did you abduct me and drag me here?" she demanded while raising a brow.

"He was just supposed to get one of Asher's guns," Davis insisted. "You weren't part of the deal. I honestly didn't know he'd brought you here until I saw you in the office." Davis frowned then glared at Asher while keeping the gun aimed at Jacey, being certain she was in Asher's line of fire to keep him from shooting. "You can just toss your gun aside, if you don't mind."

"But I do mind," Asher announced while staring at Davis with an icy look.

Jacey cast a quick glance at Asher several feet behind her. "He's not going to shoot me," she insisted then glared at Davis with a crazed look in her eyes. "Shoot him, Asher."

Davis was surprised by her words. He held the gun aimed at her with more conviction, although the fear showed in his eyes. "Drop it or she dies," he growled as beads of perspiration formed on his forehead and his finger tightened on the trigger.

"Shoot him!" Jacey shouted at Asher.

Asher and Davis stared at each other for an uncomfortable moment while Davis kept his gun on Jacey. Jacey knew her position between the two men with guns was preventing Asher from getting a clean shot. She knew she'd have to force her body to dive out of the way, but she was having a hard time convincing herself to do that. Although she was convinced he'd never shoot her, any sudden movement from her might cause Davis to pull the trigger accidentally. Asher kept his eyes locked on Davis. Asher then sneered and tossed his gun aside. Jacey groaned and felt her entire body sag with defeat. She cursed herself for not diving to the floor and letting them shoot it out. She was confident Asher had better aim and faster reflexes. Davis aimed the gun at Asher and appeared more confident now that he was the only one holding a weapon.

"Why, Davis? What made you snap?" Jacey suddenly asked, although not as fearful as she should have been.

"It pretty much began with Doyle Cobbler blackmailing the rest of us on the board as well as other prominent members at the club," Davis replied. "When he had his *accident*, we thought the blackmailing died with him. Then a month later, it started up again. It didn't take long for us to realize Jeannette must have found the incriminating evidence her husband left behind and decided to continue where Doyle left off."

Jacey stared at Davis with surprise. "You mean you killed Jeannette? That was you I ran into at the house?"

"No, I didn't kill Jeannette," he remarked. "My partner was upstairs. He killed Jeannette. I was looking for the evidence Doyle had over us when I ran into you."

"Why Brian and the other board members?" Asher asked as he moved closer to Jacey from behind.

Jacey tensed at Asher's closeness to her. She knew he was putting himself into position for an attack. She panicked at the thought. The moment she was out of Davis' line of fire, Asher would be gunned down.

"Brian's death is a little harder to explain," Davis remarked but refused to elaborate. "It wasn't until Nathan found blackmail evidence in Brian's office at the museum that we realized it had been you and Brian behind the blackmail and not Jeannette. Unfortunately, Nathan tried to extort money from me to keep quiet about other information he'd discovered as well. Carl revealed that information to me. I couldn't risk it getting out, so they both had to go."

Asher appeared dumbfounded while staring at Davis just over Jacey's shoulder. "Brian and I weren't blackmailing you," Asher boldly announced. "That's ridiculous!"

"Don't bother denying it," Davis launched back. "Brian was blackmailing you, so you'd help him financially destroy the rest of us. That's why he wanted you on the board, so you'd side with him. For all I know, you were actually the one who murdered Brian, so he wouldn't tell Jacey the secret you'd been keeping."

Jacey glanced at Asher and raised her brow in question. He caught her look.

"It's not important right now," Asher informed her while keeping his attention on Davis.

"Brian witnessed a fight between Maxwell and Asher," Davis boldly offered, answering her silent question. "Asher admitted he'd been in love with you for years, and Maxwell threatened him to stay out of your lives."

Jacey stared at Davis in silence and with little emotion. Apparently, he was expecting a bigger reaction, or any reaction from her. She didn't bother to mention that she already found out, since its significance was irrelevant now.

"The blackmail had to stop," Davis insisted. "Brian's gone, so that only leaves you, Asher. Unfortunately, arranging for you to have an accident wouldn't be nearly as easy as it was with Doyle. Taking you down required a lot of planning and a lot of collateral damage." He then looked back at Jacey. "I'm sorry you had to get in the middle of this, Jacey, but there's no turning back now." Davis drew a deep breath then exhaled and looked back at Asher. "This is how it's going to go down. You went over the deep end after discovering Nathan was not only blackmailing you with the evidence he found in Brian's office, but he'd also been secretly seeing Jacey. When you came down here to confront him, you discovered Nathan and Jacey hooking up. It's really a clever plan, if you ask me," he remarked. "Everyone knows how jealous you are over Jacey and how you hated Nathan. The police will have no trouble believing you killed them in a fit of jealous rage over their affair."

"Huh? Pity no one's going to believe that," Jacey announced while raising her brow. "Unfortunately, the lab tests will show that I'd been with Asher earlier. Enough people will vouch that I was a virgin when I broke up with Maxwell. I wouldn't doubt forensics would reveal I'd lost my virginity as early as this afternoon." She shook her head. "No, it'll be hard to make your story stick against DNA and forensics."

Asher's eyes didn't leave Davis despite Jacey's remarks. Davis appeared surprised and looked at both.

"There's no way. You two wouldn't--" Their looks told him it was true. Davis suddenly sneered possibly due to more than just crushing his fictional story. "You certainly ruined that plan, but it doesn't change the end result."

"No, just makes it sloppy," Asher bluntly informed him. "You'll look suspicious no matter what story you tell now."

"No matter. There won't be anything left of this place," Davis announced. "It's as Jacey suspected. I'm going to burn it and all evidence to the ground. It's the only way to be sure. There's just one loose end I need to tie up."

Davis aimed the gun at Asher and squeezed the trigger. Jacey cried out and leaped in front of Asher. The bullet hit her in the chest and threw her backward into him. As Asher caught her, he was unable to contain the horror on his face.

"Jacey!"

As she collapsed to the floor, Asher sank to the floor with her. Davis stared with horror at the fallen woman in Asher's arms. For a moment, he appeared almost as stunned as Asher. Anger crossed Davis' face, and he again squeezed the trigger, wanting to kill Asher for his own blunder. The gun clicked empty. Davis groaned and took two quick steps toward Asher. Asher sprang to his feet with rage and was prepared to fight. Davis struck him on the side of the head with the gun. Asher collapsed to the floor near Jacey while clutching the cut on his temple. Davis sneered at the fallen man and shook his head.

"I wanted *you* dead," Davis lashed out. "I never wanted to see Jacey harmed. It's your fault she's dead!"

Asher continued to clutch his head while attempting to focus on Davis, but he was unable to move from the floor. Asher watched helplessly as Davis set fire to a bag of shredded paper in the aisle then piled boxes of files near the burning bag. The boxes quickly caught fire. Asher looked at Jacey where she lie and pulled himself closer to her.

"Oh, Jacey, no." He gathered her into his arms and sobbed softly. "No, Jacey. No!"

Asher continued to rock her in his arms while sobbing. When he looked up, Davis was standing over him. Several feet behind Davis was Asher's gun, partially hidden beneath one of the shelves. He only eyed it a moment then looked up at Davis, who stood over him.

"I'm not stupid," Davis scoffed lowly while glaring at him. "I won't allow you the opportunity to get away. I know your reputation too well."

Davis revealed the baton style flashlight and coiled back to strike him where he knelt with Jacey partially on his lap. Asher suddenly jetted upward like a striking rattlesnake and tackled Davis across the room. They crashed into several bags of shredded files. Asher punched Davis several times with accurate hard hits then pulled him to his feet and resumed the beating with a sharp, fast kick in the chest then alongside his head. Davis was thrown backward again. Asher grabbed him by the throat with his left hand and slammed him violently against the wall. Asher coiled back with his flattened palm and sneered.

"If I'm going to hell, I'm taking you with me!"

Asher was about to deliver a deadly blow when someone struck him in the face, throwing him back. Nick stood over Asher as Davis nearly collapsed to the floor from his brutal beating. Nick frowned while glaring at Davis and shook his head with disgust.

"You fool," Nick snarled at the older man. "You should know better. You'll ruin everything. Get yourself cleaned up and join the others outside before you're missed."

Davis slowly straightened and staggered up the stairs. Nick approached Asher, who seemed more than slightly off balance. He bled from the head and swayed while breathing heavily, unable to focus on the large man. Nick threw a punch and struck Asher in the face. Asher stumbled backwards and fell against the wall past where Jacey lie. Nick pulled a knife from his pocket and approached him. Asher could barely stand without clinging to the wall. He glanced at Jacey's motionless body on the floor just behind Nick then glared at him, showing little emotion.

"What's wrong? Can't take me in a fair fight?" Asher snarled while breathing heavily.

"The legendary Konrad Asher," Nick announced with a teasing grin. "Toughest son-of-a-bitch in the entire town. Don't seem so tough now, huh? Maybe love's made you weak."

"No, the concussion made me weak," Asher remarked. "Love gives me the strength to kill you."

Asher breathed heavily and wiped the blood from his temple. He slowly straightened and composed himself. Although he looked ready for a fight, it was doubtful he could maintain his balance for more than a moment. Though he possibly only needed one moment.

"Do you think by beating me you'll be more respected--more feared?" Asher demanded.

"You're the most feared person in town," Nick announced casually while grinning. "Beating you will make *me* the most feared."

Asher again looked behind Nick. The file boxes toward the back were now swiftly burning and the flames were rising higher. It wouldn't be long before the room was engulfed in smoke and flames. Asher met his stare, smirked, and chuckled lowly.

"But I'm not the most feared, and I'm certainly not the most dangerous," Asher casually informed him. "What motivates a man is what holds the power."

Nick appeared confused then angry. Asher struggled to maintain his balance while clinging to his bleeding head as he breathed heavily.

"I've heard enough from you," Nick announced with a sneer, clearly annoyed. "Quit stalling. You won't get the chance to recover."

Asher attempted a smile and clutched the nearby shelf for support. "I don't need to recover to defeat you," Asher informed him. "The most dangerous person I know is standing right behind you." His grin was mildly unsettling and almost certainly psychotic. "And *she* looks really pissed."

Nick stared at Asher while attempting to understand the comment. He uncertainly glanced to the floor behind him. Jacey was gone! Nick instinctively turned. Jacey stood directly behind him with a bitter, hateful look on her face. She suddenly spun into a roundhouse kick and struck him on the side of the head. Nick was thrown several feet, dropping his knife. He caught his balance and looked at Jacey with surprise as he straightened.

"You're supposed to be dead!"

Jacey lifted her shirt to reveal the bulletproof vest from Asher's closet with the name 'Asher' embossed on it. Her look remained venomous.

"Yeah, well, I keep some bad company," she snapped.

Jacey kicked him again. Nick blocked the kick and caught her ankle, proud of his fast reflexes. Jacey tossed herself to the floor and kicked with her other foot, striking him in the face. Nick stumbled backward from the severe blow. Jacey rolled across the floor, sprang to her feet, and continued with a series of wild kicks. Nick managed to block one of several and punched her in the chest. Jacey was thrown back, startling her. She caught herself then straightened and smirked while indicating the bulletproof vest.

"Nice try," she scoffed then attacked him with several more kicks.

Nick was thrown back several steps with each kick. Asher clung to his shelf and watched with a tiny, satisfied grin. Jacey glared at Asher as she blocked Nick's fist.

"What the hell are you smiling at?" she demanded then returned to the fight at hand.

Nick suddenly tackled Jacey to the floor, straddled her waist, and placed his hand on her throat, attempting to strangle her. Jacey bit his hand until he screamed and released her. She punched him harshly in the mouth, rammed her knee into his groin, and heaved him off her. Nick clutched himself in agony. Jacey scrambled to her feet.

Asher smiled and chuckled. "That's my girl."

Jacey looked at Asher and gave him a tiny smile and a wink. Nick pulled himself to his feet.

"Behind you," Asher casually announced with a slight gesture of his finger.

Jacey barely looked behind her as she spun into a kick, casting Nick backward and to the floor. He hit the floor harshly and appeared momentarily dazed. He grabbed the discarded knife, sprang to his feet, and lunged for Jacey. Asher leaped to the floor, grabbed his discarded gun partially beneath the shelf, and flipped himself into a sitting position with the gun aimed. Jacey saw Asher with the gun aimed as Nick lunged for her. She let out a startled scream and leaped out of Asher's line of fire. The second she was clear, Asher pulled the trigger, shooting Nick directly in the forehead. Nick was thrown backward and to the floor, possibly not knowing what even hit him. Asher collapsed against the bags of shredded files with an exhausted groan. Jacey slowly lifted herself to her hands and knees and stared at the dead man. She raised a brow with a cold expression.

"Nothing personal, Nick," she snarled.

Jacey slowly pulled herself to her feet and looked back at Asher with a tiny smile.

"Nice shot--considering your condition."

Asher groaned and attempted to sit up straight. He managed a weak smile. "Don't tell anyone I'd been aiming for his chest," he announced. "I didn't mean to take away your fun, but the smoke is getting thick in here, and I felt we should move things along."

Both looked at the rapidly burning files. Jacey hurried to Asher's side and helped him to his feet.

"Good thinking," she replied as he leaned on her. "I think we'd better go."

"Just when we were starting to have fun," Asher teased.

Chapter Thirty-seven

Timon entered the reception office and paused within the doorway. He grimaced at the sight of Carl's outstretched hand, knowing the man in Nathan's office doorway was dead. Timon nervously crossed the reception office and slowly approached the body just beyond the doorway. He stepped through the office doorway, crouched alongside Carl's body, and cringed while reaching into his jacket pocket, feeling for a cell phone while attempting to avoid touching any blood. He gingerly removed Carl's cell phone then exhaled with relief. He quickly stood and turned. Monroe was standing directly behind him with his gun aimed. Timon suddenly cried out, stepped backwards, and stumbled over Carl's body. He fell to the floor, looked at the body, and screamed again while scrambling to his feet. Monroe clutched his head while unsteadily holding his gun. Timon once more stared at Monroe and groaned.

"Damn it, Monroe," Timon cried out. "Where the hell have you been?"

"Some bastard coldcocked me. Locked me in a closet." Monroe lowered the gun and nearly dropped it. He stared at Timon with concern. "Is help on the way?"

Timon lifted the phone in response. "Angel was supposed to call the police for me, but you can never tell with that one. I thought I'd make certain and call them myself. I need to get help then find Jacey. I'm convinced she's doing something stupid as we speak."

"Where's Jacey now?" Sheriff Monroe asked.

"I have no clue," Timon replied then hesitated and looked around. "Do you smell smoke?"

"Probably from me," he announced. "I was in the smoking lounge for over an hour." Monroe extended his hand to Timon. "Give me the phone. I'll call for help. You just get yourself out of here in case the killer's still running around. If you see anyone else, get them out as well."

Timon uncertainly handed Monroe the cell phone. "What do you intend to do?"

"I'm going to find Jacey," Monroe replied. "Go on, just get out of here."

"You can barely stand on your own. How do you expect to find Jacey?" Timon asked then appeared sympathetic toward the injured sheriff. "Let me help you outside. I'll look for Jacey and Asher."

Monroe pressed several buttons on the phone then eyed Timon. "I'm a tough bastard," he grumbled. "I'll be fine. Just go."

Monroe was about to speak into the phone when he suddenly swayed and collapsed to the floor. Timon watched him fall and land on the floor with a thump. He stared at the fallen sheriff and blinked several times.

"Yeah, you're tough all right."

✝

Professor groaned and slowly sat up within the smoking lounge. He was obviously disoriented and dizzy from the stun gun assault. Roxy stood over him with a small revolver aimed at him. He slowly lifted his head, saw the gun aimed at his face, and then looked at her with surprise and confusion.

"I don't understand, Roxy. Why?" Professor gasped, although he didn't dare move.

"Because my father is a corrupt, manipulating bastard," she snarled. "He's been smothering me for years. He only wants to breed me with the right man, so he can have the precious son he always wanted." She sneered with disgust. "Fixing me up with that pig Brian!" She glared demandingly at him and waved the gun. "Can you believe he actually told me I should forgive Brian for sleeping with Angel? My perfect escape from that hellish relationship and he thought I should just forgive the prick." She shook her head defensively. "Jeannette was the only one who understood me, and my father took her away from me."

"What?" Professor gasped softly. "Jeannette was having an affair with you? Is that why your father killed her?"

"No, that wasn't why he had her killed, besides I'm sure he had Nick do it for him," she snarled while curling her upper lip at the thought. "He'd never get his own hands dirty."

"Then why would he kill Jeannette?"

"For the same reason he killed her husband, Doyle," Roxy proclaimed. "Doyle was blackmailing his partners and a few other club members. My father found out and arranged an accident. It was a win-win for him. Doyle's portion of the club reverted back to the surviving members and Jeannette got nothing. While I was helping her pack up some of Doyle's belongings, we discovered her husband's blackmail evidence. I talked her into continuing with the blackmail and even got my father to give her a job at the club to keep her in the loop." She frowned with disgust. "I never suspected he'd have her killed for it. That's when I decided I was bringing my father and this entire club down to their knees. They were going to pay for killing Jeannette." She snorted a laugh. "I would have loved to have seen the look on my father's face when he opened that blackmail note after Jeannette's death. I'm surprised he didn't have a heart attack."

"So you were blackmailing your own father?"

"I hated him," she lashed out. "Look at this place? Men's Smoking Lounge. I'd love to see the place burn to the ground with all those chauvinistic pigs trapped inside, lighting their cigars on the flames consuming them."

"That's dark," Professor muttered.

"I planted evidence to make sure the blackmail pointed back to Brian and Asher," she remarked. "I knew he'd love an excuse to go after Asher. He never liked the guy. I hid the evidence in Brian's office, hoping the police would find it, but Nathan got there first. I saw him sneaking into the museum that night I was there. Despite that he attempted to use it against me, it worked out better than I'd anticipated."

"Is that why your father killed Brian?"

She suddenly glared at him with hostility. "My father didn't kill Brian, I did," she snapped. "I hated him. I hated that I allowed him to put his filthy hands on me all for father's approval. I hated him for sleeping with Angel and betraying me like that. That bastard took my virginity and then turned around and slept with that slut Angel! He deserved what he got."

"Wait," Professor remarked while attempting to stall for more time. "Why did you kill Carl?"

"I didn't kill Carl," she shot back with anger. "I just needed to stay out of the way and let my father melt down. Nathan nearly ruined everything with those photos he found of me with Jeannette. The pervert actually confronted me about my affair, threatening to expose it if I didn't give in to his advances. His biggest mistake was thinking I was innocent in Brian's murder. I left the evidence Nathan used against me for my father to find. I'm sure he went ballistic. I wouldn't doubt Nathan got his. Nick probably took care of it for him. My father is probably already on his quest to deal with Asher as well. It doesn't really matter who wins. The other will end up in jail, and I'll have gotten away with murder, because everything points back to my father, Brian, and Asher. I'll finally be free from my father and inherit all his money at the same time." She then frowned. "There's only one down side to all of this."

"And what's that?"

"I didn't want to kill you, but it looks like I have no choice. You were supposed to be my ally and my alibi. You were supposed to tell everyone you suspected Asher of blackmail, but you just couldn't let go of that blind faith." Roxy aimed the gun at Professor's head and cocked it. "Sorry, Professor. I really do like you."

Roxy squeezed the trigger. He pinched his eyes shut and awaited the gunshot. A shot rang out. Professor let out a soft gasp then slowly opened one eye and looked at Roxy. She stared at Professor with a look of horror on her face. Blood soaked through the front of her shirt. Her lips parted to speak but no words came only blood seeping from her mouth. As the gun fell from Roxy's hand, she sank to the floor. Professor looked across the smoking lounge to the doorway. Timon stood in the doorway with Monroe's gun stiff in his hand and a horrified expression on his face. He stared at Roxy a moment then dropped the gun with a gasp.

"Oh, my God," he cried out while clutching his face. "I've shot a girl!"

Professor stared at Timon a moment as if uncertain how to respond to any of what had just happened. Professor released the breath he had been holding and groaned softly while forcing a smile at his friend.

"Yeah, but you saved my life."

Timon stared at Professor a moment as if unable to respond then managed a smile. "I did, didn't I?" He frowned and shook his head. "I'm going to need months of therapy."

Professor groaned and slowly pulled himself to his feet with use of a nearby chair. Timon hurried toward his side and helped him to his feet.

"We need to go back to the executive offices and haul Sheriff Monroe out of there. He has a concussion," Timon informed him. "I'm worried, because I've been smelling smoke, and it's getting worse."

"If there's a fire, wouldn't the alarms sound?" Professor asked.

"Jacey thinks someone disabled them, so they could shut off the security cameras. Considering someone murdered Carl, that's a pretty good assumption." Timon then hesitated. "I hope Jacey's okay. She went after Asher. If something's happening, you know it's happening around Asher. We should look for her."

"Let's get to Sheriff Monroe first," Professor announced. "We should call the fire department just to be safe. They were supposed to respond to the earlier alarm, according to Angel, but I haven't heard the siren."

Timon flashed Carl's cell phone he held. "Let's call them and find out."

"Call them on our way to the offices."

Chapter Thirty-eight

Smoke from the file room fire was already starting to creep its way up to the first floor. It wasn't much of a surprise that the fire alarms didn't sound or that the sprinklers didn't turn on and douse the flames. Jacey helped Asher past the open reception office door. She happened to look inside and saw Monroe lying unconscious on the floor not far from her desk. Jacey released Asher in the doorway and hurried to Monroe's fallen side. She gently tapped his face until he woke.

"Monroe, are you okay?"

Monroe moaned softly then stirred and nearly sprang to his feet. Once he realized who was standing over him, he stared at Jacey and appeared almost angry.

"Where the hell have you been?" the sheriff demanded, startling her.

"You're feeling your old self," Jacey muttered. "I'd say you're going to be fine."

Asher looked out the doorway then back at them. He clutched his handkerchief to his still bleeding head then glanced at the bloody rag. He tossed the handkerchief aside and stared at Jacey, who helped steady Monroe.

"Do you think you can get Monroe out of the building?" Asher questioned.

She suddenly glared at him with annoyance. "Where the hell do you think you're going?"

Asher smirked, possibly at her spirited attitude. "Just need to tie up a loose end."

Jacey straightened while carelessly releasing Monroe. Monroe collapsed to the floor with a thud and a painful groan. She took two quick steps toward Asher in the doorway.

"Konrad, you're not going after Davis," Jacey cried out with a look of hostility on her face.

"Konrad?" he remarked with surprise and grinned teasingly. "I must be in trouble."

"In case you've forgotten," she remarked and indicated the smoke wafting along the ceiling, "the building is on fire. We need to get out of here now."

Asher indicated the sheriff on the floor. "You just get Monroe out of the building," he insisted in a calm, reassuring tone. "The fire department should be here soon. They'll handle the fire." He flashed a charming smile. "I'll meet you out front in five minutes."

Jacey was about to protest when Asher quickly kissed her on the lips and left the office area. He seemed more energetic than he had been just three minutes ago. She sometimes wondered what motivated him. Jacey glared demandingly at the barely conscious sheriff still on the floor.

"Aren't you going to stop him?" she exploded.

Monroe rolled his eyes and groaned while attempting to sit up. "Sorry, I was too busy bleeding," Monroe muttered. "He knows what he's doing. Best just to stay out of his way and let him do it."

Jacey groaned and helped Monroe to his feet. Both appeared to be in some agony.

"You're just as bad as he is," she huffed.

They hurried to the reception office doorway as fast as possible with Monroe hanging heavily on her shoulder. As they stepped into the back hallway, they could see the walls and floor near the back glowing as smoke billowed from the closed file room door. Both shared the same expression of concern. A hasty exit seemed like a good plan.

"Ah, hell no," Sheriff Monroe murmured.

He attempted to pick up his pace despite his unsteadiness, throwing Jacey off her feet and into the nearby wall. They struck the opposing wall with a loud thump. Jacey could feel the heat coming from the wall against her shoulder, causing alarm to spread through her. She pulled away from the wall and attempted to straighten Monroe.

"Work with me, Sheriff," she boldly announced. "Slow and steady."

"We don't have time for slow and steady," he blurted out and again attempted to hurry.

Timon and Professor rounded the corner from the distant main hallway, saw them, pointed, and then ran for them. Jacey was relieved when both men each took an arm and helped tow the injured sheriff toward the main hallway.

"Where's Asher?" Timon asked while looking around with concern.

Jacey frowned and stopped to look around the back hallway. "He's around *somewhere*."

The back wall and file room door were now engulfed in flames. Jacey's expression dropped at the sight. Professor released Sheriff Monroe, took a quick step back to her, and firmly grabbed her arm.

"Don't even think about going anywhere but out the front door," Professor snarled at her, showing hostility for the first time. He forced her to follow Timon and Monroe.

†

Davis ran across the boardroom, approached one of several filing cabinets, and routed through several drawers. Smoke had now reached the boardroom as well, rolling across the ceiling like a rogue fog. He removed a small stack of files, stuffed them into a briefcase, and shut it. He touched his bruised and bleeding lip tenderly then turned. Asher casually leaned in the doorframe with his hands in his pockets and stared at Davis with a slightly mocking smile on his face.

"We didn't get a chance to finish our earlier conversation," Asher announced and gently pushed the door shut with his foot, blocking most of the smoke and Davis' only exit.

Davis stared at Asher a moment with surprise, took a step back, and attempted a nervous smile. "What, uh, happened to Nick?"

"He underestimated the wrath of a woman," Asher proudly replied.

He continued his approach toward Davis with a pleasant and charming appearance yet a nerve-wracking calmness about him. Davis appeared increasingly nervous.

"When someone tries to kill me, I don't take it personally," Asher informed him. His look turned angry. "Trying to kill Jacey, well, that just plain pisses me off."

Davis reached into his briefcase, removed a semiautomatic, and aimed it at Asher. He seemed less tense and more confident now that he held the gun.

"You made a big mistake coming back for me," Davis informed him. "This time I intend to finish what I started."

Asher studied the gun a moment. His expression remained casual and almost humored as he locked eyes with the man aiming the gun at him.

"Yeah, Davis," Asher announced simply. "Me too." His smile increased. "Incidentally, semiautomatics work better without the safety on."

Davis' expression suddenly dropped. He fumbled with the safety.

†

Just outside the swiftly burning country club, dozens of drunken men sat on the front lawn while singing songs as they passed a bottle around. They didn't even appear to notice the building was on fire. Fire truck sirens were heard in the near distance and gaining. Timon helped Monroe out of country club through the front doors with Professor nearly dragging Jacey behind them. Jacey looked back at the building and stared with horror at the flames jutting from the second story as well as the first floor. It wouldn't be long before the fire spread to the front of the building, blocking the main entrance and anyone left inside.

"Oh, my God," Jacey gasped, unable to take her eyes off the country club.

None had realized how quickly the fire had spread. Timon and Professor now turned and stared with shared looks of horror as well.

Timon glanced at Professor and appeared alarmed. "Think we should go back inside and look for Asher?" he gasped.

"We wouldn't know where to start," Professor informed him. "He could be anywhere."

They heard a gunshot from the second floor furthest away from the fire facing the parking lot. Everyone gasped and looked at the building with surprise. Glass shattered from the second floor window. Davis flew backwards through the window and fell two stories to the parking lot below. He landed on Brian's Corvette roof with a loud crash, demolishing the top of the car. There were several gasps. The car alarm sounded upon impact. Jacey, Monroe, Timon, and Professor all stared at the demolished sports car with the limp, broken man lying on top of it.

"Damn, I liked that car," Timon remarked.

"I guess we know where Asher is," Monroe muttered while shaking his head.

As the police cars and fire trucks approached, their sirens wailing loudly, Monroe motioned for Timon to help him greet the approaching vehicles. Jacey turned toward the country club and ran for the front doors.

Professor suddenly grabbed her around the waist, catching her, and stopped her from achieving her mission. "No, no, no. You're staying right here."

"But Asher--"

"--will kill me if I let you go back in there."

Jacey appeared concerned and anxious while watching the burning building. She fought Professor's hold around her waist, but the fire kept her preoccupied. The higher the flames rose, the harder she pulled against him. Jacey was consumed with concern for Asher. Without warning, she rammed her elbow into Professor's ribs, forcing him to release her. She ran for the building. The front door to the country club opened, causing her to stop suddenly. Asher passed through the doorway with a bottle of champagne and two, long stemmed champagne flutes. Jacey appeared relieved and nearly sank to her knees. Asher approached the crowded parking lot, raised the bottle, and smiled at her. Jacey gathered her strength and ran to him. The building suddenly exploded and rocked the entire estate. Asher continued to walk casually toward Jacey as if he hadn't even noticed. Everyone else within the parking lot screamed and took cover behind several cars. Jacey ducked with surprise then stared past Asher at the burning inferno. Flaming debris rained down across the parking lot. Asher stopped before Jacey and smiled charmingly, indicating the bottle of champagne.

"Almost forgot the champagne."

Jacey stared at the burning building with her mouth partially open then looked back at Asher and his charming smile. She groaned softly, threw her arms around his neck, and held him.

Chapter Thirty-nine

Almost every light inside and outside the museum seemed to be lit. Several cars were parked out front, including Jacey's jeep and Asher's SUV. Professor and Timon sat at the bar within the game room. Both had drinks in their hands and matching solemn looks on their faces. Professor gingerly touched his bruised head and sipped his club soda.

"What a night, huh?" Professor remarked. "Clubbed over the head, tased into a twitching mess, and nearly killed by a beautiful woman." He groaned softly. "Guess that's as close as I'll ever get to a date around here."

Timon snorted a laugh while sounding slightly drunk. "I don't know what you're complaining about. I *shot* a beautiful woman tonight. You know I'll *never* get a date in this town."

"Yeah, but your chances of that were pretty slim to begin with," Professor remarked with little emotion.

Timon glared at Professor, taking offense to the remark. Asher and Jacey sat on the sofa in an intimate embrace. Jacey rested her head on Asher's shoulder while he held her and played with the small bandage on his temple. Timon casually turned around on his bar stool and stared at them with a tiny, humored smile.

"You know, Asher," Timon announced. "I'm starting to see why no one invites you to parties. Have you ever gone anywhere without killing someone or blowing shit up?"

Asher glanced at Timon with his usual, casual smile. "Maybe once."

Timon chuckled softly.

Asher looked back at Jacey and smiled warmly. "Well, what do you say? Ready to go home?"

Professor turned on his stool and looked at them with a curious stare. "You know, you two have been pretty cozy over there."

"Yeah, I don't know why you two don't just get married and get it over with," Timon announced in a drunken tone.

Asher glanced at them and smiled knowingly. He looked back at Jacey. "That's a terrific idea. What do you say to that?"

"I'm free tomorrow," she announced teasingly, although mostly serious.

"Then it's settled," Asher announced cheerfully. "We'll get married tomorrow." He looked back at Timon and Professor, who stared at them with baffled looks. "Jacey and I are going to Bermuda tomorrow afternoon and get married on the beach. Who wants to come along? My treat."

Professor and Timon stared at them with surprise in a moment of awkward silence. Both men then raised their hands and grinned.

The End

Other books by Holly Copella!
Reviews left on Amazon are appreciated!

"The Battle for Andrea María"

A cruise ship attack turns six survivors into overnight celebrities after they take credit for the heroic act of a stowaway who died saving them.

The cruise is just what Jess needed--a bit of harmless fun far from her daily grind. But what begins as a relaxing vacation turns into a desperate fight for her life when terrorists take over the ship and start piling up bodies. Teaming up with a mysterious stowaway, Jess attempts to send out a distress call but knows they cannot wait for help to come. If she or the few remaining passengers have any hope for survival, Jess must act now. The papers dub it "The Battle for *Andrea María*," but to Jess it is the moment she fought side-by-side with her enigmatic Romeo, saving the ship--and losing him. She thinks the story ends there, but really, the nightmare is just beginning...

"Insanely Deadly"

When the dead return to life, it's up to an admiral's daughter and a mildly insane, former war hero to save their small town.

Jetta Cross, a Navy Admiral's daughter, is tasked with keeping her father's comrade, a former war hero turned town crazy, grounded in the real world. Capt. John Hunter is still fighting the war in his head, where imaginary dead people are part of his world. When a viral outbreak brings about a zombie uprising, Hunter is left to his own devices. He must resume his role as a one-man commando unit in order to destroy the ravenous undead. With Hunter still fighting his own inner demons as well as the undead, the townspeople fear their zombie neighbors may not be the only threat. Stranded at the island's luxurious resort with a handful of workers, Jetta is forced to live up to her father's reputation and take charge of the deteriorating situation at the hotel. She must wage her own war against the infected before the government declares her hometown a total loss.

"Deadly Institution"

A town recluse suspected of killing his wife teams up with a young woman in order to stop a killer.

After being accused of murdering his wife, Konrad Asher turns his back on the town that once adored him. Ten years later, he still holds his grudge and the title of the most feared man in town. With the reopening of the burned mental institution, where his wife had died, former employees are now murdered one-by-one, throwing suspicion back on Asher. A young local reporter, Jacey, is forced to reveal her long-time friendship with the infamous recluse in order to clear his name not only in the recent murders but to exonerate him in the death of his wife as well. Will Jacey's relationship with Asher invite the killer closer to her? Or is the killer already in her life?

"Screenplays: The Island Collection"
"Jungle Princess", "A.L.F. Resort", "Brighton Island"

Discover how romance and fun in the sun can be downright *chilling*!

"Jungle Princess" is a romantic/thriller that leaves a teenage girl stranded on an island with two male shipmates and a creature of "unknown" origin. She soon discovers the island is home to an abandoned prison with several prisoners roaming free. What really killed over one hundred prisoners? And is it still out there--?

"A.L.F. Resort" is a romantic/thriller set on an island resort with Artificial Life Forms as the main draw. At this resort, all your fantasies come true...until a malfunction removes safety inhibitors on the A.L.F.'s. Zombies, biker gangs, and mobsters run amuck, turning fantasies into nightmares. A young reporter gets more of a story than she anticipates, but will she survive long enough to write the story?

"Brighton Island" is a romantic/thriller set on a private island. When the owner's niece brings her psychic friend to the mansion, his presence awakens the spirits' tortured souls. As the psychic attempts to solve the old murders, the niece is confronted with the possibility that she's next to join the mansion ghosts. Stranded on the island with a crazed killer, her uncle wages his own war to save them. Will his "shock and awe" tactics actually save them or get them killed?

"Reaper of Souls"
A fantasy short story

A young woman must outwit an evil sorcerer in order to save her brother or become one of his minions forever.

Unwilling to believe her brother is dead, Reggie discovers an underhanded deal made with Kahn, a less than ethical sorcerer, who collects humans to serve as slaves in his kingdom. In order to rescue her brother from his horrible fate, she must complete his failed task or be forced to serve Kahn forever. After being transported to his world, Reggie realizes that even if she beats Kahn at his own game, she's at his mercy for him to uphold his end of the deal. All seems lost until Kahn's discontented, self-serving brother, Helsing, arrives. Can Reggie convince Helsing to help her? And at what cost?

"Death Displacement"

A grief-stricken man travels back in time to seek revenge on the woman who murdered his girlfriend but inadvertently falls in love with her.

Kane is about to marry the woman he loves. His life is perfect. A few weeks before the wedding, a vindictive woman from his girlfriend's past mysteriously arrives and kills her. He learns of a traumatic accident that happened five years earlier, which triggers Riley's hatred for his girlfriend. Distraught over his girlfriend's death, Kane uses an antique time machine to travel into the past in order to find and destroy the woman responsible. When he runs into Riley's younger self, he realizes she's not the monster she later becomes, and he can't bring himself to destroy her. With a little help from his oddball friend from the past, they formulate a plan to prevent the accident that sends Riley down her destructive path. Kane's plan backfires when he falls for the younger Riley. His new tortured existence is further complicated when future Riley, his girlfriend's killer, shows up with her own devious agenda that doesn't include him. Will he be able to stop the time ripple, which ultimately ends with his girlfriend's death? Or will future Riley take him out of the timeline forever--

"Dead Village"

After strange happenings isolate a small resort town from the rest of the world, nearly one hundred residents seek refuge at the closed hotel. Only eight survive the night. And that's just the beginning...

One day after the entire population of Fox Ridge Village disappears, a car wreck forces several unsuspecting crash victims to seek help at the closed summer hotel. Within the hotel, they discover the grisly aftermath of a brutal slaughter. Crash victims Vander and Devon, a reluctant clairvoyant, team up to solve the riddle of the "haunted hotel" and the mass hysteria plaguing the remaining survivors. By the time they discover the hotel's secret, they're already drawn into the hysteria. As the body count continues to climb, it's a race to isolate the source and bring everyone back to reality before they kill one another. Will Devon be able to communicate with the traumatized spirits before their fate becomes her own?

"Misfits, Inc."

A seemingly ordinary, young woman meets four misfits who claim she has given them supernatural powers.

While on a business trip to a remote island paradise, a bored secretary, Hailey, has her world turned upside down when her path collides with a psychic freak, Skyler. He attempts to convince her that they had met in his dreams, and she had chosen him as one of her four mystic warriors. After Skyler foresees a woman's death, they discover an unidentified creature has killed one of the guests. They are joined by a lounge pianist and a rich playboy, who also claim they had met her in their dreams. If Skyler's prophecies are genuine, the evil entity controlling the ravenous creatures needs to destroy Hailey to ensure its survival. Reluctantly accepting her fate, Hailey has to locate the last and most powerful of her chosen warriors, The Guardian. Their fate is in doubt when The Guardian turns out to be a self-absorbed, former cat burglar with a bad attitude. Can Hailey turn her company of misfits into an elite team of mystic warriors? Or will The Guardian's secret agenda destroy them all?

"Basement Dwellers"

A viral outbreak at a hospital leaves a mortician, sheriff, and coroner fighting for their lives against a horde of undead and the CDC.

After a massive car wreck leaves several survivors in critical condition at the local hospital, a surgeon uses experimental drugs on his critical patients and accidentally causes a zombie outbreak. When local mortician, Lexx, receives an infected corpse as her client, she becomes stranded in the hospital basement during CDC quarantine along with the local sheriff and the coroner. The infamous surgeon struggles to find a cure for his infectious blunder by using the other survivors as test subjects. Meanwhile, Lexx and the sheriff attempt to locate his missing sister, who's stranded somewhere in the battle zone that once was the emergency room. It's a race against time and the ravenous undead. Can they survive the undead before CDC sanitizes the hospital of all infection?

"Witness Protection"

After witnessing an execution, a resourceful young woman attempts to disappear while being pursued by a hitman and a handsome federal agent.

A helicopter pilot, Jackie Remus, reluctantly agrees to go on a date with one of her clients, but her date is unexpectedly cut short when she witnesses a man being murdered. After narrowly escaping with her life, she is placed into protective custody. When the safe house is breached, Jackie makes a daring escape from both the hired killers and the handsome FBI agent, who wants to return her to protective custody. With a little help from her sly and crafty friend, Monroe, Jackie is convinced she can disappear until the trial. While on her journey to meet with her friend, she solicits help from a few shady but lovable characters along the way. Although she manages to stay one-step ahead of the hired killers, the federal agent remains in hot pursuit. Will Jackie reach Monroe before she's captured by the FBI and returned to protective custody? Or will the hired killers silence her first?

"Town Darling"

After surviving a brutal attack that claims the lives of those she loves, a young woman seeks revenge on a corrupt town.

Going back home is never easy, but for Casey, it means returning to her corrupt hometown where she barely survived a brutal attack. Accompanied by two family friends, she seeks justice for the night that destroyed her life. Her physical scars are nothing compared to her emotional ones, forcing the local sheriff to believe that the town darling is back for revenge. As the conspiracy for her revenge appears to be leading up to the coveted town fair, the sheriff is determined to stop her from fulfilling her vengeful scheme...but guilt over his role on that fateful night continues to haunt him. Will his desperate need for Casey's forgiveness be his undoing? Or will Casey's desire for revenge destroy them both?

"Unconditional"

A young woman puts her life on hold to care for an unstable, highly skilled combat soldier, who believes someone is trying to kill him.

A botched military coup leaves a team of elite fighters injured with one clinging to life in a coma. When Harlan wakes from his coma, he's left with no memory of his past life. His commander's daughter, Indy, takes it upon herself to care for the fallen war hero. She's challenged with more than just his physical care as she combats with not only his memory loss but also his newly found desire for her. His infatuation with her becomes the least of her worries when he sinks back into his role of a combat soldier. Believing his life is in danger, his fighting skills surface, turning him into an unpredictable and dangerous man. Will his memory return to him before Indy is forced to commit him? Or will he finally find his nemesis, "the coyote", and possibly claim the life of an innocent person?

"Witness Protection 2"
The Return of Whiskey Tango Foxtrot

Believing she holds the clue to millions in missing laundered money, a young woman is placed into the protective care of a former Navy SEAL team.

Feeling sorry for her recently separated co-worker, Leeann invites Wiley to join her and her friends on their night out. Little does she know that finding her co-worker murdered is just the beginning of her nightmare. Leeann unknowingly holds the key to fifty million dollars in potentially laundered mob money. With hired killers pursuing her, the FBI places her into a different kind of protective custody. Former Navy SEAL team Whiskey Tango Foxtrot reunites to keep Leeann alive at their secret hideaway. What should be an easy assignment takes an unscheduled turn when secrets, lies, and betrayal threaten to derail their mission. Is the team prepared for a war on their own doorstep? Will Leeann's misguided trust endanger the lives of those sent to protect her?

Coming Fall 2016!
"Witness Protection 3"

ABOUT THE AUTHOR

Holly Copella has been writing since the age of twelve when her frustration at a book's poor plot drove her to author her own story. Over the last decade, she's written a number of screenplays, some of which she's now adapting into novels. Her fascination with zombies and other darker material lends an edge to her writing, which tends to lean toward horror. As a fan of Agatha Christie, she appreciates the craft of a good plot and the importance of creating significant characters.

Hailing from Pennsylvania, Copella lives in the Endless Mountains on a farm with her rescue horses and other animals. In addition to writing and reading fiction, she enjoys riding horses and traveling to Las Vegas and Disney World.

www.ingramcontent.com/pod-product-compliance
Lightning Source LLC
Chambersburg PA
CBHW061155170626
46809CB00003B/1105